Chapter 1

Having spent the day providing entertainment for the residents of Whistling Pines Senior Residence, I was prepared for a quiet dinner with my family and watching G-rated television shows appropriate for my middle-school son. I'd just set a tater-tot hotdish (aka Minnesota comfort food) on the table as Jenny placed our daughter, Amy, in her highchair.

A disturbing commotion coming from our next-door neighbors distracted me. I hurried to the window as our son Jeremy rushed past the table and stood next to me with his nose pressed against the dining room window. We watched two volunteer firemen pull the loading ramp down from a U-Haul truck parked in front of the neighbors' rental house.

"Is the fire chief moving out?" Jeremy asked.

"I doubt it. Sparky just moved in," Jenny replied.

The question was answered when Wendy, the fire chief's very pregnant girlfriend and my co-worker at Whistling Pines, pulled up behind the moving van in

Acknowledgements

A special thanks to Brian Johnson whose zany suggestions helped me develop the plot, create the characters, and add seasoning to the boiling caldron of ideas. Madeline Jarvis and Shannon Walz suggested North Shore locations and allowed me to use their names as my fictional librarians. Deanna Wilson proofs the roughest first draft. She corrected plot, cop, character, and legal mistakes while suggesting changes that made the book better. As always there are a legion of additional people who contribute to my books. Julie continues to endure my distracted writing while she keeps the house and family together. Natalie Lund, the sentence structure and preposition rule enforcer, marks up a later draft and improves the readability of the book. Anne Flagge and Deanna Wilson make a final post-editing sweep to catch the last typos, and truncated words. Without their dedicated assistance, the books would be much less than they are. Finally, thanks to Jude Pittman and Susan Davis of BWL Publishing for your editing and continued support.

Dedication

To Tom Norton

*"Marriage is an alliance
entered into by a man who
can't sleep with the
window open, and a
woman who can't sleep
with it closed."*
-George Bernard Shaw

Table of Contents

her purple Pontiac. She immediately started directing the firemen as they unloaded her furniture from the back of the truck.

"It appears Wendy is moving in with Sparky," Jenny remarked as she snapped a bib on Amy. "I thought she'd planned to delay living together until after the wedding."

Scooping the steaming hotdish onto our plates, I said, "Wendy mentioned something to Kathy Christensen about her lease ending. She and Sparky decided she should move in with him now rather than renewing her apartment lease."

"That makes sense," Jenny replied. "I wonder how Sparky's mother feels about that?"

Jeremy, still enthralled by the movers, unknowingly answered the question with, "Some old lady just parked in our driveway. Uh oh. She's yelling at the firemen who've stopped carrying furniture."

"Jeremy, come to the table and eat before your dinner gets cold," Jenny said.

"No, Mom," Jeremy replied as he pointed to the unfolding scene next door. "Dad had better go out there. I think there's going to be a fight!"

Dropping the serving spoon, I joined Jeremy at the window. Having left her car idling in our driveway with the door open, Sparky's mother was now in front of a fireman, sticking her finger into his chest while gesturing toward the truck with her other hand.

"What do you think she's saying, Dad?"

Although I didn't read lips, I could tell that every other word she yelled started with the letter F. "Stay here with Mom." I headed for the back door.

The moving stopped when two firemen set a dresser down on the sidewalk while they awaited directions to either reload the truck or continue moving furniture into the house. Sparky's mother turned her ire from the firemen to Wendy as I trotted across the yard.

"Listen, you...harlot! You are not moving in with my son before you're married! It's bad enough that you tricked him into impregnating you. There is no way I'm allowing you two to live in sin before the sacrament of marriage!"

Wendy got into her future mother-in-law's face. "Harlot? I'll have you know that this child was not created by divine intervention. Your innocent little boy was a willing participant in the creation of this kid, who is your grandchild." She pointed to Sparky, who was hiding just inside the rental house's front door. "Sparky, m up. Get your butt out here and tell your mother what's happening!"

After a gentle shove from Stella Hygge, a female firefighter, Sparky stumbled down the steps. Regaining his balance, it appeared he was weighing the wisdom of intervening or running away from a confrontation between his mother and his fiancée.

"Go on, Sparky," Stella urged from the steps. "You're almost forty. Stand up to your mother."

It was obvious that standing up to his mother wasn't one of Sparky's life skills. He skulked to the small group of us while we awaited his words. "Mom, Wendy is moving in with me." He brushed the toe of his shoe at an imaginary rock without making eye contact.

Sparky's mother froze, then turned to Wendy. "This is all your doing! My son has never addressed me like that before. He's always been a good boy who's done what I've told him to do."

An unusual weather pattern had delivered sauna-like heat and humidity to Two Harbors, leaving us all on edge and drenched in sweat. The whole town was irritable, with Wendy already at her limit before Viola Johnson, Sparky's mother, appeared. Wendy's face went from red, to redder, then to the shade of cooked beets. "Listen, Viola, I'm moving in today. The 'sacrament' of marriage isn't going to change the fact that I'm pregnant, or that I'm moving in with your son."

"Noooo!" Viola wailed. "You can't move in or have the baby before you're married. You have to put the father's name on the birth certificate. If you're not married, you'll have to list the baby's father as 'unknown.'"

The firemen, aside from being hot and sweaty, appeared amused. I sensed the confrontation moving toward an irreversible conclusion, so I stepped between Viola and Wendy. "Listen, the wedding will formalize what's already happened. Wendy and Sparky are in love, and their child will be born to loving parents who lived together before the wedding took place. It's the twenty-first century and there are new societal norms."

Viola glared at me, then looked at Sparky. "Well, what do you have to say for yourself, Roland?"

Stella Hygge started to laugh. "Sparky's name is Roland?"

Her laughter broke the tension and Viola took a deep breath. "Roland, say something."

"The baby is mine, Mom. Wendy isn't a harlot."

Pointing to Wendy's swollen abdomen, Viola asked, "How did *this* happen?"

Wendy rolled her eyes and said, "In the usual way. He put his..."

I jumped in before Wendy supplied the details of the impregnation. "Listen, Viola, if you want to be a part of your grandchild's life, you have to make peace with Wendy and Sparky. Leave the past behind and look ahead. You'll have a cuddly baby who you can spoil. That child will be the next generation of your family, and he or she should be accepted with love, regardless of when, where, or how the conception occurred."

"Wait?" Viola said. "Is there something about *where* he was conceived that I should know about?"

Aware that I'd said something entirely out of school, I tried to backpedal. "That's what I'm trying to say. The circumstances are irrelevant."

Chuckling, one of the firemen whispered to his friend, "The backseat of that fire truck will never be the same."

Viola spun and glared at the two firemen, then turned back to Sparky. "You took that harlot's virginity in the back seat of a fire truck?"

The laughter was contagious, and even I couldn't help but laugh. Apparently, everyone but Viola knew that Wendy's virginity had been *taken* long before Sparky was in the picture.

"What's so funny?" Viola demanded.

I took Viola's arm and led her back to her idling car. "Go home and cool off. Focus on the wedding plans and having a grandchild who will arrive shortly after the wedding."

Viola composed herself. "Well, my friends told me that every baby after the first one takes nine months. The first child is often born a little early."

I watched Viola back out of the driveway and thought, *Yes, this first child will be about eight months early.* Turning back toward the rental house, I watched the firemen pick up the sofa and carry it toward the steps. Stella had her arm over Wendy's shoulders and was apparently offering words of encouragement, while Sparky had a deer-in-the-headlights look. With things apparently under control, I walked home.

Jenny placed my plate into the microwave as I walked in the back door. She started the cycle, then hugged me. "It appears you defused the situation, Peter."

"For now. I'm afraid there might be a repeat performance."

"What was Viola's problem?"

"She called Wendy a harlot and accused her of seducing Sparky." I paused. "Then someone let slip that the baby might've been conceived in the back of a fire truck."

Jenny chortled. "In the back of a fire truck?"

"I think her words were 'took Wendy's virginity in the back of a fire truck.'"

"Viola thought Wendy and Sparky were virgins? They're both in their thirties!"

Jeremy interrupted the discussion after apparently overhearing too much of our whispered adult conversation from the dining room. "What's a virgin? Our olive oil is virgin. Is that like organic?"

Grimacing, I replied, "Something like that."

Chapter 2

The television meteorologist predicted no break in the weather pattern that was pulling hot, humid air into northeastern Minnesota. Later in the week, a cold front would sweep in from Manitoba, causing thunderstorms and the potential for tornadoes. In the meanwhile, Two Harbors' natural air-conditioning, supplied by southeasterly winds sweeping across Lake Superior, was staying offshore. Instead of saving to buy ice fishing augers, snowmobiles, and snow blowers, North Shore residents were now buying the limited supply of window air conditioners that had been collecting dust in retail storerooms and warehouses.

That unwelcome weather news meant another day of dealing with cranky old folks who had little tolerance for anything out of the norm. I shared the forecast with Jenny as I poured coffee for her. She sighed and closed her eyes. "Can you show a movie today or do something to keep the residents distracted?"

"It's not our usual movie day."

Due to the heat and lack of air conditioning in our house, neither of us had slept well despite having the windows open. Jenny, who has an immense capability to mask her irritation, lost it. "I know it's not our usual movie day. Can you do something extra today to keep the residents entertained? Everyone will be tired, hot, and sticky, leading to grumpiness and arguments. If you can keep a bunch of folks distracted, that will mean fewer people bugging my nursing staff with questions about heat rashes and irritable bowels."

"Are people more prone to irritable bowels during hot spells?"

"No. People are more irritable about their bowel issues when it's hot."

Not catching the full depth of Jenny's irritation, I didn't let the topic drop. "I thought people were always unhappy with their bowels. I mean, it's one of the usual topics of conversation after grandchildren, the weather, and poorly fitted false teeth."

Taking down a box of cereal and a bowl, Jenny seemed to ignore me until she suggested, "Why don't you go to work early?"

"Why?"

"So, the police won't arrest me for killing you in the kitchen."

Finally getting the message, I took a step back, out of reach in case she chose to swing a frying pan at me. "Sure. I'll check into the Netflix movie options."

*　*　*

Waving at the receptionist as I entered the lobby, I was stopped by a man unpacking tools near a newly donated upright piano in the residents' lounge area. "Can I help you?" I asked.

"I'm the piano tuner," he replied. "I don't really need any help."

I watched as the man removed a felt strap and a long wooden-handled wrench that I recognized as a piano hammer. He opened the upper portion of the piano, exposing the strings. After isolating some bass strings using the felt, he played a few notes, and then looked at me. "I take it this hasn't been used in a while?"

"The piano was just donated to us. I really don't know its history. I played a few keys and knew it was badly out of tune."

Playing middle C, the piano tuner put the wrench on a tuning nut and wiggled it until satisfied with the tone. After that, he played a chord and adjusted the other strings until they were all in tune.

"I've seen people use electronic boxes to tune," I said as he switched keys.

"Amateurs often rely on electronics. I prefer to tune by ear."

"I assume the tuning will go better if I don't interrupt you."

The man smiled. "Thank you."

I entered the dining room and drew a cup of coffee before walking to a table where

Mary Gilbert, Karla Telker, and Kathy Christensen were seated. "May I join you?" I asked, while pulling back the empty chair before waiting for a response.

Hearing the piano tuner make adjustments, Mary cringed. "It's like listening to fingernails on a chalkboard," she said as the man adjusted a badly out of tune string.

"Who donated the piano?" I asked.

"Astrid Tostenrud bequeathed it to Whistling Pines," Karla replied. "She used to be the organist at the Methodist Church."

Mary cringed as another off-key note was struck. "Was she deaf before she died?"

"I think she was more broke than deaf. She lived off social security, and I don't think piano tuning fit into her meager budget."

"I'd quit playing before I'd use a piano out of tune," said Mary, who'd been a piano instructor and church organist.

Karla raised her eyebrows. "I think she played at church. Maybe she'd quit practicing at home."

Finishing the higher register keys, the tuner moved to the left end of the keyboard. The first key he struck made a very strange buzzing sound. The next key just thumped. I looked at Mary. "That sounded bad."

"Someone must've dropped some debris inside the piano."

A moment later, the piano tuner walked into the dining room and looked around. Seeing me, he approached our table. "I assume you have something to do with the management here?"

I stood and smiled. "My lack of gray hair gave me away?"

"I'd like to show you something," he replied, gesturing toward the door.

The trio of women followed us across the lobby to the residents' lounge. A faded dusty cloth, tied with string, sat on the piano bench. Handing the box to me, the piano tuner said, "Based on the dust, it looks like it was sitting on a ledge inside the piano and must've fallen onto the wires when the piano was moved. I thought you might be able to find the owner."

The package was about the size of a recipe card box. Setting it on a nearby card table, I untied the string and pulled back the dusty fabric, exposing a wooden box with beautiful parquet inlaid wood. Turning it to inspect all the sides, I frowned. "There's no opening."

"Is it solid or hollow?" Kathy asked.

"It's light," I replied before gently shaking it. "And there's something rustling inside of it."

Kathy put her hand to her mouth. "Astrid had a cat."

Grimacing, I set the box down. "It's too small for her cat."

Kathy waved off my comment. "Maybe she had Tabby cremated and sealed the ashes in the box."

"Why put it into the piano?" I asked as the tuner resumed his work on the other side of the room.

"It's probably something she wanted to keep hidden," Karla suggested. "Maybe it contains a treasure map."

I gently shook the box again. "I think it sounds more like paper than ashes. But, why put papers in a box, then glue it shut?"

Seeing us gathered around the card table, Howard Johnson, the self-appointed Whistling Pines Mayor, asked, "What's today's project?"

"There was a wooden box inside the piano," I replied.

Cocking his head, Howard looked at the box. "I saw puzzle boxes like that when I was stationed in Japan."

"What's a puzzle box?" I asked.

"There are sliding panels on the sides, top, and bottom. When you move the correct combination of panels, in the correct order, the box opens." He bent over the box. "May I handle it?"

"Sure," I replied.

Running his fingers over the surface, Howard turned the box all around. He placed his thumbs on the two inlaid end panels and pushed them. They slid outward about a centimeter. "There you go," he said, handing the box back to me. "All you have to do is determine where the other sliding panels are, and in which order they have to be moved to open the box."

As Howard walked away, I wrapped the box back in the fabric. "I'm going to talk to the director to see if there is a family member who should get this."

Kathy shook her head. "Astrid never had any children. I don't recall her having any family after her husband died."

Mary nodded her agreement. "Astrid always referred to the church's congregation as her family."

Karla had been listening and thinking. "I recall her mentioning cousins, nephews, and nieces to the choir once. So, she had some family."

The piano tuner approached us and smiled. "I hate to be rude, but it's more difficult to tune when you're here talking."

* * *

I took the puzzle box to my office and closed the door before booting up my computer and entering my password. A quick search for puzzle boxes yielded an array of boxed jigsaw puzzles offered by a dozen online vendors. Re-entering the search for Japanese puzzle boxes gave a different set of jigsaw options, plus a link to an online auction site where I found a similar box. The ad said the shipment would include directions for the twenty-seven steps required to open the box. A second box advertised a seven-step combination. That ad included the description, *Himitsu-Bako*.

Entering those words in my search description yielded pages and pages of Japanese puzzle box photos, along with the explanation that the original wooden puzzle boxes had been developed in the *Hakone* region of Japan. Known for the variety of wood and the skilled artisans, the puzzle boxes were a way of showcasing the artistry and craftsmanship of Japanese woodworkers.

Sadly, the information didn't include a universal set of instructions for opening puzzle boxes. If anything, it seemed that the potential combination of anywhere from seven to thirty-three sliding panels could include a nearly infinite number of combinations, with some panels sliding out, then in, then farther out, then back in, when manipulated in the proper sequence with the other sliding panels on the sides, top, and bottom of the box. After closer examination, I found four additional sliding panels on the opposite side of the box. None of the moves opened the box, nor did they seem to affect the motion of the other panels I found.

Deep in thought, I was startled when my office door opened without anyone knocking. Oblivious to my irritation at the interruption, Brian Johnson stepped in and sat down in my guest chair. His cherubic smile turned to a frown when he saw the puzzle box in my hand. "That's one of those Oriental toy boxes, isn't it?"

"According to the internet, it's a Japanese *Himitsu-Bako* box."

"My cousin was stationed in Okinawa when he was in the Marines. He sent one to me for my sixteenth birthday."

"I hope it came with instructions," I replied.

"It did, although the panels got a little sticky in the Minnesota humidity. May I give it a try?"

I handed the box to Brian, who turned it end to end before sliding the panels. After a few moments, he found a combination that allowed him to slide the entire top open a fraction of an inch. Handing it back to me, he said, "There."

I slid the top back and forth, but it never opened more than a sliver. "It's not opening any farther."

"You'll need to find a combination of other panels to open it the rest of the way."

"What other panels?" I asked, looking at the ends of the box.

"I don't know. They're there somewhere, although they may be a little sticky in this humidity."

Setting the box aside, I asked, "Did you know Astrid Tostenrud?"

"The crazy cat woman who was the organist for the Methbyterian Church?"

"What's a Methbyterian Church?"

"The Methodists and Presbyterian congregations were dwindling, so they decided to merge."

"And they chose to call themselves the Methbyterians?"

"Probably not officially. That's the name that the Lutherans gave the merged church. I assume the congregations involved chose to associate themselves with one or the other of the two denominations. As a Lutheran, I fail to see the difference in their theology. They're both derived from the..."

Hoping to salvage my original conversation, I asked, "Did you know Astrid?"

"No, I never met her."

I grimaced. "You knew all about her, from the cats to which church she played in, but you've never met her?"

"What can I say? Two Harbors is a small town."

"We found the box inside a piano Astrid donated to Whistling Pines."

Looking at the box, Brian sniffed his nose. "Was it wrapped in that dusty cloth that's making my nose run?"

"Yes."

"I suppose she didn't place it inside the piano just before she died with the intention of you finding it."

With my patience running thin, Brian's statement of the obvious irritated me. "I'm sure she didn't."

Brian straightened as if he'd had a sudden insight. "Did I tell you why I started playing the tuba?"

"No."

He broke into a broad smile. "I was into heavy metal."

Groaning, I tipped my head back. "I thought we were solving the puzzle box mystery."

"It seemed like we needed something to break the tension." He pointed to a notepad on my desk. "You should write that joke down for your son."

"I don't think he'd get the heavy metal reference."

Brian frowned, then lifted his eyebrows. "Why was the tuba player standing on his front steps? He couldn't find the key."

"Again, that may be a little over Jeremy's head."

Undeterred, Brian went on to the next joke. "My neighbor knocked on my door at 3 AM. Luckily, I was still awake playing my tuba."

Chuckling, I wrote that joke on my notepad. "I'm not sure Jeremy will get it, but it'll make Jenny laugh."

Standing, Brian nodded. "Good!" Halfway through the door, he turned back. "There is an easy way to open the box."

"Really?"

"A big hammer," he replied as he disappeared.

"I may resort to that," I responded to the empty door. "But I think I'll leave that as my last option."

I was carrying the box to the director's office when Lee Westfall interrupted halfway down the hallway. "Is there any chance you can take a group of us to that new fast-food place?"

Not recalling any recent construction in Two Harbors, I asked, "Which place is that?"

"It's the one I've been seeing advertised on the cable networks. They have a hedgehog mascot. It's a clever name."

"A hedgehog mascot?"

"Yeah. I keep laughing about the two guys arguing in the car about the new burger."

Still confused, I asked, "Where is it located?"

"Being a local, I thought you'd know."

"Not really."

"It must be busy. They advertise every fifteen minutes."

"I can't think of any restaurants with a hedgehog mascot."

Jeri, Lee's wife, walked up to us. "What are you two up to?"

"I was trying to get Peter to take us to that hedgehog restaurant."

Jeri frowned. "Hedgehog restaurant?"

"The one they're advertising on CNN."

Recognition swept Jeri's face. "Sonic."

Lee snapped his fingers. "Yes!"

"There aren't any Sonic restaurants in Two Harbors," I explained.

"Dang it! Their burgers sound really good. And that hedgehog..."

Chuckling, I continued my trip to Nancy's office. She was reading an email on her computer and turned when I knocked on her doorframe. "Hello, Peter."

Setting the box on the corner of her desk, I said, "We found this in the piano that was donated to us."

"What is it?"

I slid the end panels to demonstrate their motion, then said, "It's a puzzle box. Apparently, each has a unique set of slides and combination of moves that allows it to open. I don't know how to open this one."

Nancy accepted the box from me and shook it gently. "There's something inside of it."

"Yes," I agreed, "there seems to be something hidden inside of it."

"The piano was donated by Astrid Tostenrud. I wonder if she hid the box in the piano to hide something?"

"Or, was it put there by whoever owned it before Astrid?"

Nancy slid the box back to me. "Do we think there's anything valuable inside?"

"I have no idea."

Nancy leaned back. "It's probably not a bomb."

"I'm pretty confident it won't explode," I replied. "On the other hand, it could be something of historical significance."

"It's the size of a recipe card box. Maybe Astrid hid her favorite Christmas cookie recipe inside it."

"Who donated the piano?" I asked. "Was it a bequest in her will?"

"Astrid left her estate to the merged Methodist/Presbyterian church. The parish council chairman offered it to us since the church already owns a piano, and none of the members were interested in it."

I chuckled. "That church only has about twenty members, and the youngest of them is about eighty years old. They were probably relieved to find someone who would *move* the piano."

Nancy clasped her hands and leaned forward. "Why don't you make it a challenge for the residents. At the next gathering, announce the discovery of the box and offer the residents a chance to solve the puzzle combination. It might provide days of entertainment."

I stood and picked up the box. "That's a wise suggestion. I'm planning to show a movie this afternoon. I can explain the mystery box before the movie starts. I'll set it on one of the card tables in the community room and anyone who is interested can try to open it."

As I stepped out of Nancy's office, I bumped into Sherry Vogel, my new assistant. Sherry, full of youthful enthusiasm, smiled at me. "What's the recreation plan for today?"

"Post an announcement that we're showing a movie this afternoon."

Sherry stared at the box. "What's that?"

I explained the discovery and the puzzle aspect of the combination to her.

"Do you think there's money inside of the box?"

"I doubt it. The owner wasn't rich."

* * *

Feeling a bit uneasy about the murky provenance of the box, I called the Two Harbors police chief. "Hi, Kerry. I have a mystery."

"Is there an actual crime involved in your mystery?" the police chief asked.

"I don't know yet."

Kerry sighed. "Call me back if you determine that a law was broken."

"What if I found something valuable but can't establish ownership of the item."

"What did you find?"

I explained the box, its discovery, and our plans for revealing the contents.

"I suppose anything valuable would belong to the church that donated the piano to you. Although, I suppose the contents of the piano could be considered part of the gift." Kerry paused. "Let me know if you uncover a crime or find something inside the box other than a shopping list."

"I'm not sure we can get the box open to determine what's inside."

"You're creative. I'm sure you'll come up with something."

As I ended the call, I realized Sherry had entered my office and was staring at me. "Is something wrong?" I asked.

"Do you have more popcorn stashed somewhere?"

I handed Sherry a keyring and said, "There's more in the locked cabinet in the community room."

Sherry took the keys, then paused. "Did you have a particular movie in mind for this afternoon? One of the men suggested, *Cat on a Hot Tin Roof* in honor of the heatwave."

"I think he was kidding. I thought we'd watch *The African Queen*, with Humphrey Bogart. It's always a hit."

Sherry lurched forward after being shoved from behind. Regaining her balance, she stepped aside as Hulda Packer plowed her walker into my office. "Where's the damn box from the piano?" she asked as she pulled a hammer from the shopping bag hanging on her walker.

"Please put the hammer away," I said.

"I heard there was a cash prize for the person who opened the box."

"There is no cash prize, and we're not going to smash the box to open it."

"I walked all the way down here only to have you change the rules and eliminate the cash prize?"

"There's never been a cash prize, Hulda. Besides, the box is a work of art. We're not going to smash it open. I hope someone will be able to find the correct combination of slides and pulls to solve the puzzle."

"There's a puzzle inside of it?"

"Opening the box is the puzzle," I explained. "I don't know what, if anything, is inside of it."

Hulda banged her walker into Sherry, the furniture, and the walls as she yanked it back and forth to turn around in my cramped office.

Sherry yelped when Hulda scraped her knee. Rubbing the scrape as Hulda left, Sherry asked, "Has she always been so..."

"Irritable," I suggested.

Sherry nodded. "All of the other words I came up with were inappropriate for our workplace."

Laughing, I said, "Really? I didn't think a minister's daughter would know words like that."

"Peter, I rode the school bus for twelve years, then spent four years attending a public university. I know lots of swear words."

"But you don't use them."

Sherry's face reddened. "Not here."

I gestured for her to leave. "Go start the popcorn. I'll be down with the box in a few minutes."

I'd just shut down my computer when I heard footsteps approaching. Wendy swooped into my office and sat in the guest chair. "Call your friend, the police chief."

"What happened?" I asked as I took out my cell phone.

"I'm going to kill Sparky's mother." When I froze, she added, "It may be justifiable homicide. I'd like his opinion on how to best stage it for an insanity defense. I assume the jury will take into account my raging pregnancy hormones."

"I've never heard of hormonal imbalance as a murder defense."

"Temporary insanity, then."

I sat, realizing this wasn't going to be a quick discussion. "What's going on?"

"Viola is upset because Sparky moved out. She shows up at the rental house every night with supper for him."

"You're over there most nights. Do you have a problem with her bringing you meals?"

"She only brings enough for Sparky, not both of us. He's gentlemanly and shares, but she's starting to get under my skin." Wendy paused and relaxed slightly, "And her choice of foods is atrocious! I mean, not every dish in her cookbook has to contain cabbage, beans, cauliflower, or Brussel sprouts, does it? There are foods that don't produce gas or cause indigestion. A pizza wouldn't kill her, would it?"

"I assume those are rhetorical questions."

Struggling to push herself out of the chair, Wendy waved off my help. "Thanks. I needed to vent."

"You're not going to kill Viola now?"

Wendy paused at my door. "Not now. Probably not until tonight."

"Don't kid about murder. If something happens to Viola, you'd feel terrible."

"I really wouldn't," Wendy said as she walked away.

I was almost to the community room when my cell phone rang. Stepping to the side of the hall, I answered, "This is Peter."

"Have you checked into Astrid Tostenrud's death?" Brian Johnson asked.

"Um, not really. Why?"

"I heard a rumor that she died in a suicide pact."

"What are you talking about, Brian?"

"She made a deal with one of the other organists that if one of them was dying of a terminal illness, the other would kill them to save them from suffering through a prolonged illness."

"Where did you hear this?" I asked.

"From a voice in the next booth at the Log Jam Café."

"Who was speaking?"

"I don't know. I have a stiff neck and I couldn't turn around. Besides, it's impolite to stare at people in restaurants. Didn't your mother ever teach you that?"

"I generally disobey that rule when I overhear people talking about committing crimes."

"I suppose there's some merit to that. Although listening in on a couple of hitmen talking about someone they killed might be inadvisable."

"Brian, you overheard a discussion about two organists with a suicide pact. I don't think that discussion would get you killed."

"People are always looking for an excuse to kill a tuba player. I try not to antagonize anyone."

"You antagonize your wife and neighbors by practicing day and night. You antagonize me with crazy conspiracy theories and sick tuba jokes. There must be others I've overlooked."

Brian chuckled. "Maybe there are people who have good reasons to murder me. Just the same, I don't listen in on people plotting or discussing my death."

"I've got to go. Goodbye, Brian."

I was disconnecting my call when Ginny Johnson, who suffered from dementia, put her hand on my arm. "Peter, I'm so glad I found you. Did you hear that the church bell ringers killed Astrid Tostenrud?"

"Bell ringers?"

"You know, the people who ring the steeple bells."

I tried to envision the very small church steeple. "I think there's only room for one bell in their steeple, and I think it's actually electronic."

Ginny appeared confused. "Maybe I saw that in a British mystery on television. Was Astrid's throat slashed in the belfry?"

"I honestly don't know how she died."

"Check it out. I recall the vicar finding her body. If she wasn't killed in the belfry, the murder I saw was probably in the Lutheran church or on television."

"I don't think the local Methodist/Presbyterians refer to their spiritual leader as 'the vicar.'" I took Ginny's elbow and steered her down the hallway. "Let's go watch a different movie. I think we're showing *The African Queen*."

"I love Humphrey Bogart," Ginny said. "He was quite a hunk, and a gentle, thoughtful lover, too. I really miss him."

I shuddered at the thought of Ginny being so confused. Then I remembered that she had lived in California while her husband was stationed in San Diego. "Tell me more about Humphrey Bogart."

"I met him in between his marriages to Lauren Bacall..."

My mind drifted to previous conversations with Ginny. She couldn't remember anything new, but her memories of the past were often quite lucid. *Did she really have a fling with Humphrey Bogart?*

Chapter 3

Once I'd shown the moviegoers the puzzle box and explained my interest in having them help find the solution that opened it, I stepped outside and called Kerry Stone.

"Have you opened the box?" he asked.

"Not yet. But I've had several interesting conversations about Astrid Tostenrud's death. What do you know about how she died?"

"I don't know anything about how she died. Actually, I don't know about many deaths unless they involve a car accident or some other trauma."

"So, she wasn't murdered?"

"Why? Was there something suspicious about her death?"

"Depending on who I've spoken with, she was either the victim of a suicide pact or was killed by Methodist or Lutheran bell ringers."

"Today is not April Fool's Day."

"I know that. I'm just telling you that her death may have been suspicious and deserves your attention."

"Are you being serious, or are you repeating the demented ravings of one of your senior lunatics?"

"It's sometimes hard to tell the difference, isn't it?"

"Peter!"

"I don't know. One of my sources is somewhat credible."

The line went quiet for so long I thought Kerry had hung up, or we'd been disconnected. "I'll find her death certificate and check with the doctor who signed it. Okay?"

"Thank you."

"This is all stirred up because you found the box in the piano, right?"

"I guess so."

"Open the box. That might settle all of the speculation."

"I'm working on it."

"Call Ray Gradien. He'll be able to open it."

"Isn't he the old locksmith?"

"Yes. He's helped us out a couple of times."

"The box isn't really locked, per se. It's a puzzle box opened by sliding little wooden slats back and forth."

"Humor me. Talk to Ray."

After disconnecting Kerry, I looked for locksmiths in Two Harbors. *Ray's Lock and Key* was the only local listing. I touched the phone number on the website and the phone was answered almost immediately.

"This is Ray, how can I help you?"

"I'm not sure you can. I'm Peter Rogers from Whistling Pines Senior Residence. I have a Japanese puzzle box without instructions and I'd like to see what's inside it."

Ray chuckled. "Let me guess; Chief Stone suggested my service."

"That's right!"

"To be honest, my specialty is dealing with traditional locks and opening locked cars. A puzzle box would be a stretch."

"I thought Kerry's suggestion was a bit outside the box, so to speak."

"Do you know what's inside the box?"

"It was found inside a piano that's been donated to us. The piano's owner is dead, and she left us no clues about the box. I'm not even sure she was the one who left it inside the piano."

"You're at Whistling Pines, right?"

"Correct. I'm the recreation director here."

"I'll be replacing the locks in a house near you tomorrow. I can stop by and take a look at your box after I'm done. I make no guarantees about being able to open it, but you've piqued my curiosity."

"That's great, Ray. One more person's opinion will be helpful."

I ended my call with the locksmith and looked up as Wendy approached me, yet again. Her advanced pregnancy caused her to walk leaning backward to counterbalance the baby bump, now the size of a beach ball. Her forehead was beaded with sweat, and her breathing labored.

"What's up?" I asked. "Have you decided to go with the temporary insanity defense?"

"This mother-in-law stuff is stressful. How do you guys deal with it?"

"I love my mother-in-law, and she's been nothing but supportive and..."

Wendy cut me off before I could finish the sentence. "That's you. How does Jenny feel about your mother? Did they get along before you married her?"

I flashed back to my mother's early inappropriate comments about Jenny being the unwed mother of a young son. "They started out a bit rocky, but my mother was the person who handed me an engagement ring to present to Jenny."

"How did they turn the corner and become friends?"

"I think Mom got to know Jenny. Once they'd spoken, Mom realized how sweet and wonderful Jenny was. But Mom struggled to understand my role with Jeremy because I wasn't his biological father. Once I adopted Jeremy, it was clear that he was my son, regardless of the biology."

"Viola is unhappy that I got pregnant before the wedding."

"Trust me, once she holds her grandchild in her arms, all will be forgiven."

"We know the baby is going to be a boy. That was obvious in the last ultrasound."

"That's great. Has Sparky told Viola that?"

Wendy shook her head. "We're waiting until after the delivery. We have to agree on a name."

"Choosing a name from Sparky's family will go a long way toward breaking the ice with Viola."

"We *are not* naming the baby Roland Junior."

Nodding, I said, "Maybe you can use Sparky's father's name as the baby's middle name, or maybe use Viola's maiden name as the baby's middle name."

Wendy shuddered. "Sparky's father was named Hangensfjord. Everyone called him Hank."

"The kid would be twenty before he could spell that. How about Viola's maiden name?"

"Lawton-Campbell is a little long for a middle name."

Checking my watch, I said, "You'll come up with something. The movie is about to end, and I need to get back to the community room." I was about to take a step when I paused. "You said Sparky's mom brings him dinner every night. Why don't you invite her over for supper?"

"Peter, I don't cook, and Sparky always eats his mother's cooking."

"Buy a rotisserie chicken and corn on the cob. All you'll have to do is boil water."

"I can do that! There's a guy selling fresh sweet corn by Culver's."

Humphery Bogart and Katharine Hepburn were just pulling themselves ashore on an uninhabited island after blowing up the German patrol boat when I walked into the room. I flipped on the lights as the movie credits started to roll. Sherry, who had tears in her eyes, jumped up and turned toward the door. Wiping the tears away, she smiled when she saw me.

Walking to the front of the room, I whispered, "You'd never seen "The African Queen" before?"

"I hadn't."

Ginny Johnson rushed forward and clutched my arm. "Wasn't Humphrey wonderful? He was a bit older when we were an item, but he still had the swagger and good looks. He was a little uneasy about my height. He wore lifts in his shoes when we went out together so he looked taller."

Sherry's eyes went wide. "You knew Humphrey Bogart, the actor?"

Ginny raised her eyebrows suggestively. "I *knew* him, in many ways. He was a considerate lover."

Sherry looked at me, unsure she understood what Ginny was saying, then unsure if she believed what had been said when I nodded.

"It was a May/December romance," Ginny explained. "I was young and impressionable. He was older and worldly. I might've married him if not for Katharine being in the picture."

"Excuse me," I said to the residents as people started to stand. "If any of you have a thought about how to open the puzzle box, I'd love to have you give it a try."

Howard Johnson stepped forward and extended his hand. "Can I have another look at it?"

I gave the box to him, and he turned it around many times, examining it from every angle. "I'm baffled by it," he said, handing it back to me. "You must be on the right track because you've got the lid to slide over a bit."

When no one else approached me with suggestions about opening the box, I helped Sherry pick up spilled popcorn, then we straightened the rows of chairs. "I think there's money inside the box," Sherry suggested as we finished with the chairs.

"There might be," I replied. "On the other hand, why put money in the box? It's not like it's secure from theft."

"Maybe it was intended as a gift for someone, and it fell into the piano by accident."

Our conversation was interrupted when my cell phone rang. "This is Peter."

"I found Astrid's death certificate. It says she died of complications from Chronic Obstructive Pulmonary Disease. It was signed by Doctor Fuller."

"Is there any chance she was killed by an organist?"

"What in hell are you talking about?"

"Brian Johnson said..."

Kerry cut me off. "Hold on. You're getting murder clues from the tuba player?"

"He's a good source of local information."

"He's a nut!" Kerry replied. "I mean, he's funny but I wouldn't make an arrest based on one of Brian's tips."

"What would the complications of COPD be?" I asked rhetorically. "As I recall, the patients lose lung capacity and struggle to breathe. I think they either die of pneumonia or are unable to get enough oxygen to keep their bodies going."

"I suppose that sounds reasonable."

"Was there an autopsy?"

"Most elderly people with evident health problems don't get an autopsy."

"Did you leave a message for Dr. Fuller?"

"No."

"Would you call and ask him if Astrid's death was at all suspicious?"

"Peter, I have better things to do than follow up on the apparently normal death of an elderly woman."

After ending my call with Kerry, I walked to the dining room and found a few of the residents gathering outside of the entrance, ahead of the supper seating. Karla, who was capable of holding both sides of a conversation, was talking to Lee Westfall, who was smiling and listening patiently.

"Excuse me," I said, interrupting Karla's monologue. "Lee, aren't you and Jeri members of the merged Methodist/Presbyterian Church?"

"We are, although we don't get there very often anymore. It's easier to find a ride to one of the Lutheran churches."

"I understand that Astrid Tostenrud was your organist."

"Yes. She was dedicated. Did you hear that she died during a service?"

Surprised by that news, I said, "I hadn't heard that."

"Yes, she was playing "Onward, Christian Soldiers" and was really getting into it. She gasped, then just tipped over." Lee paused. "It was a very rousing rendition, and it took the choir a couple of bars before they realized she'd stopped playing."

Karla nodded in agreement. "That was quite a service. Even the Swedish Lutherans were talking about Astrid's final performance."

Confused, I asked, "It was so memorable that the Lutherans were discussing it?"

"Well, yes," Karla said, seeming surprised I hadn't heard about it previously. "Pastor Bob announced hymn 89, "Joyful, Joyful, We Adore Thee." The congregation had their hymnals open and were ready to sing when Astrid apparently got confused and started playing "Onward, Christian Soldiers.""

In agreement, Lee added, "We all know both songs, so we all started singing the new song. Astrid was really getting into it, and the tempo kept getting faster and faster."

"Didn't that seem odd?" I asked.

"Well, it was a little strange. Although Astrid sometimes got the hymns mixed up and played them out of order. Or she changed an unfamiliar song to something she remembered if the pastor had chosen something she didn't like."

"Astrid was a bit of a traditionalist," Karla said. "She didn't like the modern hymnal."

"And the choir just jumped in?" I asked.

Lee nodded vigorously. "They seemed to think it was funny. I remember that a couple of them were giggling while trying to find hymn 575, "Onward, Christian Soldiers.""

I tried to envision an organist confusing hymns, especially changing out the scheduled song for something entirely different. "Did Astrid have dementia?"

"She seemed pretty with it," Lee replied. "She was a bit of a rebel, but she had her wits about her."

Karla put her hand on my arm. "I think all the churches broadcast and record their services for their homebound members. You can probably watch the service on the church's website."

"When did all this happen?" I asked.

"I think it was the Sunday before the 4th of July. Yes, I remember the pastor announced that the men's club and

American Legion would be putting flags on soldiers' graves after the service."

The dining room doors opened, and the residents started filing in. I walked back to my office and closed the door before going to the Methodist/Presbyterian Church website. As Karla suggested, there was a link to view each service on the church website. I chose the June 30th service and waited while the video loaded. The service opened with a prayer request for the sick, then moved to a hymn. I fast-forwarded through much of the service and skipped the sermon. After the sermon, the pastor announced communion. There was some noise off screen, and the camera zoomed out to show the entire front of the sanctuary. Someone was leaning on the organ and speaking to Astrid as the pastor and a deacon prepared to dispense communion to the congregation lining up in the aisle. The man who'd spoken with Astrid disappeared during communion, then returned, carrying a small gas cylinder which he swapped out for the oxygen bottle strapped to a small cart positioned next to the organ. The exchange was completed moments before the end of communion and Astrid shifted on the piano bench and prepared to play.

The pastor announced hymn 89, "Joyful, Joyful We Adore Thee" and Astrid, who was visible on the fringe of the screen, turned toward the pastor and seemed to snort or laugh. The pastor, apparently confused by her response, glanced at her, but opened his hymnal, preparing to lead the congregation in song.

As expected, Astrid poised her hands over the keyboard, but instead of what had been announced Astrid played the opening bars of "Onward, Christian Soldiers." The pastor, visible on the opposite side of the screen, seemed confused, but the choir, closest to the organ, seemed amused. Several of the female choir members giggled as they joined in and sang the first verse from memory while flipping through their hymnals. The two male choir members both smiled and shook their heads while singing along.

The volume of the organ seemed to increase, and as the first verse ended, Astrid's tempo picked up, leaving the choir and congregation trying to keep up with the beat. Halfway through the second verse, Astrid started hitting the wrong keys. Undeterred by the missed notes, Astrid forged ahead, until she stopped suddenly and gasped. The choir, who were focused on their hymnals, continued to sing for a few bars before they too, stopped.

I tried to enlarge the screen and move the center of focus to Astrid but was only able to view the entire altar area. She appeared to reach for her nose, probably trying to adjust the oxygen cannula, then she slumped and tipped over. A parishioner rushed to her aid, as one of the choir members took a phone from under her choir robe and apparently dialed 911. A moment later, the camera was jostled and the broadcast ended.

I reloaded the video and fast-forwarded to the point where the man spoke with Astrid prior to returning with a replacement oxygen tank. Repeatedly playing that scene back and forth yielded little information because that action all occurred in the corner of the screen while communion was being administered. The tank exchange seemed simple enough, and the man who assisted appeared to know what he was doing.

I was startled by a knock on my door. Jenny walked in as I paused the church service. "What do you have planned for supper?" she asked, until she focused on my computer screen. "Why are you watching a church service?"

"Astrid Tostenrud is playing the organ," I replied. "Watch this," I said, restarting the video as the man swapped oxygen bottles. We continued to watch as Astrid started playing "Onward, Christian Soldiers."

"She's picking up speed," Jenny said, pushing closer to get a better view of the computer screen. "Something's wrong." Jenny gasped as Astrid hit bad notes, then stopped playing and tipped over. "Did she just die?"

"I don't know. The recording stops."

"Back up to where her oxygen bottle gets changed," Jenny directed. "I wonder if the man forgot to open the valve when he swapped bottles?"

Backing up the recording, I said, "That part of the screen is so small it's hard to see what's going on."

We watched the oxygen bottle replacement twice with Jenny shaking her head. "I can't tell what's going on."

"It's really odd that the choir thinks this is funny."

"It is rather humorous that Astrid decided to play an entirely different hymn than the pastor announced."

"Let's take my computer to the community room. I think I can project the broadcasted service on the movie screen."

In the community room, I hooked my computer to the projector while Jenny dimmed the lights. Although the image was now enlarged, the detail was blurrier than when we'd watched it on the computer monitor. After watching the oxygen tank swap and the start of the hymn, Jenny stopped me. "Something is very wrong. Go back to the oxygen tank exchange."

I backtracked the broadcast to the communion service, and we walked to the front of the room so we were close to the small corner of the screen showing Astrid being assisted with her oxygen bottle. "There it is!" Jenny said, pointing to the screen. "The replacement bottle isn't green. It's blue!"

"What's a blue gas bottle?" I asked as I pulled out my cell phone.

"I'm not familiar with the color coding of gas bottles. I know oxygen bottles are always green."

After a moment, Google displayed a blue gas bottle. "The blue bottle contained nitrous oxide."

Jenny grimaced. "That's why the choir was giggling. Nitrous oxide is used as a dental anesthetic. The common name for it is laughing gas."

I flipped phone screens to my list of contacts and touched Kerry's name. He answered on the third ring. "What's up, Peter?"

"Astrid Tostenrud's death wasn't entirely accidental."

"*Not entirely accidental* isn't part of any Minnesota statute."

"What's it called when a person inadvertently causes someone's death."

"Depending on the circumstances, it could be involuntary manslaughter, or criminal negligence."

"It appears someone switched a bottle of nitrous oxide with Astrid's oxygen tank."

"Intentionally?"

"I really can't tell."

"Hang on." I heard Kerry close a door. "You can't tell? Did you see it in a picture?"

"No, Jenny and I watched a recorded church service. Jenny noticed that Astrid's green oxygen bottle was swapped for a blue nitrous oxide bottle by one of the parishioners."

"Who made the switch?"

"I don't know. The swap occurred during communion and the camera captured the entire front of the sanctuary. The gas bottle change is only visible in the corner of the screen and the person making the change had his back to the camera."

"Was he trying to hide his identity?" Kerry asked.

"I don't think so. It appeared that he came down an aisle to the organ and was facing the altar, not the camera."

After a pause, Kerry said, "Make a copy of the video, just in case the church decides to delete it. Then, see if you can find out who swapped the bottles."

"Um, Kerry," I hesitated.

"What?"

"You're the cop. I'm just the recreation director at Whistling Pines."

"Listen, Mr. Recreation Director, I'm in the middle of something else. As I recall, your boss appointed you the police liaison. Why don't you liaise yourself over to the church and ask anyone you find who switched the bottles."

"But a crime may have been committed."

"True. And if you determine there has been a crime, give me a call and I'll rush right over."

"You're as irritating as the tuba player."

"I'm sorry. I didn't catch what you said as I was hanging up."

"I said, you should've been a tuba player."

Kerry laughed. "That's a low blow."

"I think you just made up a tuba joke. You know, they play low notes and you have to blow them."

"Tell that one to your friend, Brian the next time you see him. He can add it to his repertoire of bad tuba jokes."

"Right," I said to the dial tone.

Chapter 4

I woke when Jenny sat up abruptly. "Someone's pounding on the door."

Blinking the sleep from my eyes, I pulled on a pair of jeans and bounded down the stairs barefoot. The frantic pounding at the back door repeated every ten or fifteen seconds. Approaching the door, I heard Sparky calling my name. He was dressed in a t-shirt, red pajama pants printed with tiny fire trucks, and a pair of barn boots.

"You've got to help," he said, looking relieved to see me.

"What's wrong?"

"I need toilet paper."

I waited a beat to see if Sparky was drunk, kidding, or out of his mind.

Jenny rushed up behind me and responded, "Why?"

"We're out and," Sparky paused to look back at his house, "well, it's not pretty."

"Hang on," Jenny said before rushing away.

"What's going on?" I asked.

"Mom's got the trots and she used up all the TP."

"I'm sure the gas station has some," I suggested.

"There's no time! Mom's sitting on the pot and yelling for more TP."

Jenny ran into the kitchen carrying three rolls of toilet paper, still in their plastic wrapper. "Here you go."

"Jenny, could you come with me? Mom's darned sick and I don't know what to do."

Glancing at me, Jenny said, "Check on the kids. I'll be back as quickly as I can."

After making sure the kids were both asleep, I pulled on a sweatshirt and shoes, then walked next door to Sparky and Wendy's house. I could hear raised voices through the open front door before I reached the steps.

"...she tried to poison me!" a mature woman's voice yelled from deep inside the house.

"Is that Sparky's mom?" I asked Wendy, who stood inside the front door, staring into the living room.

Resting her arms on her pregnant stomach, Wendy rolled her eyes. "Yes, it's the old witch."

I heard Jenny's reassuring voice followed by a wail. Sparky rushed down the hall, apparently unsure of his role in the emergency. He looked at me and said, "You were an Army medic, right? Do you know how to treat dysentery?"

"I was a Navy corpsman, and dysentery wasn't a problem in the desert."

Another wail came from the bathroom followed by a stream of profanity like I hadn't heard since I was discharged from the Navy. "That harlot did this to spite me!"

"Harlot?" I asked.

"Yeah," Wendy replied. "*Mom* thinks I tricked Sparky into getting me pregnant. We had her over for supper and I tried to patch things up with her."

Sparky nodded. "Then, halfway through supper Mom turned green and ran to the bathroom. She's been ranting about food poisoning since then." He paused as another wail came from the bathroom. "Do you think I need to call an ambulance?"

"Let's wait for Jenny to make that decision."

"Will you go down and check on them?" Sparky asked.

Briefly considering the situation, I said, "No."

"No?" Wendy asked.

"I'm sure Jenny has things under control, and I don't want to intrude on Sparky's mother's modesty."

"Don't worry about that," Sparky replied. "Mom isn't much concerned about who sees her in whatever state. In the summer, she often cleans the house naked."

Knowing Sparky's mother, I found myself valiantly trying not to picture her naked. The power of suggestion was insurmountable. I immediately visualized the nude, heavyset woman, walking around the house with a feather duster. "I should go back home, in case one of the kids wakes up."

I heard the bathroom door, so I paused before exiting. Jenny, looking haggard, walked down the hallway.

"Is she going to live?" Sparky asked. "Should I call 911?"

"Whatever is in her system will work its way through. Once her cramps stop, you can start giving her an ounce of Gatorade every fifteen minutes."

"Will that happen soon?" Sparky asked.

"She said she's had cramps for almost four hours. Her system must be just about empty." Jenny looked at Wendy. "I tried to explain that whatever caused this wasn't anything you fed her. Food poisoning doesn't hit while you're eating the tainted food. The problem was probably caused by something she ate yesterday."

Wendy nodded. "Neither Sparky nor I are sick. If it was something in our meal, we'd both be ill. Not that the shrew will ever admit that."

"You don't need us anymore," Jenny said. "She's got plenty of toilet paper and she'll be better in a couple of hours."

Sparky looked unconvinced. "Um, Peter, could you stay, just to make sure Mom understands that Wendy didn't cause her illness?"

"Jenny explained that to her," Wendy said.

"It might be good if she heard it from a second person."

"She'll either believe Jenny or not. My input wouldn't add anything to the discussion."

Deep in thought, Sparky paused. "I think Mom's concealed carry permit expired, so she probably doesn't have a gun in her purse. That reduces the odds there will be a murder today."

That comment brought the church video to mind. "Do you belong to the Methodist/Presbyterian Church?"

"I'm not much of a church person."

"Did the fire department respond to the call for help at that church when Astrid Tostenrud died?"

Frowning, Sparky paused when he thought about it. "Oh, yeah. I drove over when the call came in. The firemen were doing CPR on her until the ambulance arrived a few minutes later."

"Do you remember an oxygen bottle in the church?"

"Sure, I do. The EMTs always bring one along on a rescue call. They put one of those green masks on Astrid's face while they did CPR."

"Was there another one there, next to the organ?"

"Not that I recall. On the other hand, I was kind of focused on Astrid. She looked really bad."

"Really bad, how?"

"Pale and pretty much out of it."

"Do you remember her saying anything?"

"Not really."

"Do you recall a man standing nearby?"

"Peter, the whole congregation was standing there, including the guys in the choir."

"I think the man wore a suit," I added.

"I wasn't focused on the fashions. Professionals like me are trained to focus on the patient and get them care as quickly as we can."

"Do you remember a blue gas cylinder?"

"I don't remember much about anything except managing the crowd and making sure the EMTs had a clear path."

"Okay. Thanks."

"Those were some pretty specific questions. Why were you asking?"

"I think someone swapped Astrid's oxygen cylinder for laughing gas and that's what killed her."

"Well, hell. Do you think she laughed herself to death?"

Seeing that Sparky was serious, I explained, "Pure laughing gas will cause you to asphyxiate because you don't get any oxygen."

"But you'd be happy it happened, right?"

"I don't think so. I think your brain would realize it wasn't getting any oxygen and it might set off alarms."

"I didn't hear any alarms going off at the church."

"I mean mental alarms, not alarm bells."

"Oh. That makes more sense."

"Do you remember which firemen responded to the call?"

"A couple of the guys, maybe Clarke Hall and Gordy Bishop. I think Stella Hygge was there, too."

"Thanks. I'll ask them about the gas cylinders, too."

Seeming perplexed, Sparky said, "Oxygen always comes in a green cylinder. What color is used for laughing gas?"

"Its chemical name is nitrous oxide. It always comes in a blue cylinder."

"Do you think someone confused them?"

"Blue is obviously different from green. I doubt it was an accident."

Cocking his head, Sparky asked, "Don't blue and green look the same to people who are colorblind?"

As irritating as Sparky sometimes was, he did know a lot of things and reasoned through odd bits of information. His observation was spot on. "That's an interesting point. I'll check into it."

* * *

Morning came too early, and the buzzing alarm clock woke me while I was still deep asleep.

Jenny rolled over as I turned off the alarm. "Go ahead and shower first. I'll check on the kids."

I'd read that most authors used their time in the shower to mull plots and ideas. It's the one unstructured time in their day when they're away from electronic devices and can let their minds wander. I pondered the switched gas cylinders and Sparky's observation that colorblind people wouldn't notice the difference between a green and blue gas cylinder. *Who is colorblind and had access to a laughing gas cylinder? A colorblind dentist?*

Jenny was setting out her clothing when I walked back into the bedroom. She noticed my look of consternation and asked, "What's wrong?"

"I need to find a colorblind dentist."

Lacking context, Jenny looked at me as if I had lost my mind. "Is there some reason you'd need a colorblind person to do a filling?"

"It has to do with Astrid's death."

"Ah," Jenny said, gathering her pile of clothes. "That almost makes sense."

Pulling on a pair of underwear, I heard the crunch and crinkle of breaking elastic in the waistband. "All of the elastic in my underwear and socks is dying."

"Our dryer needs to be replaced. It only has two settings: Off and incinerate. If you can focus on something besides the puzzle box, Astrid's murder, and today's movie, it'd be nice if you could call an appliance repairman."

Seizing up at the prospect of paying a repairman, I said, "Maybe I can fix it myself."

Jenny paused at the bedroom door. "You don't have the knowledge, tools, or time to deal with it. Call a professional."

Seeing the wisdom of her words, I replied as I'd learned all good husbands would when they'd lost an argument, "Yes, dear."

Smiling, Jenny stepped back into the bedroom and pecked me on the cheek. "And call soon, replacing underwear is expensive."

* * *

Upon arrival at Whistling Pines, I called Oscar's Appliance Sales and Repair from my office. Oscar, whom I'd met at the Chamber of Commerce meetings, said, "Yah, I can try to fix it. But you know most of those modern dryers are full of electronics that aren't repairable. You might be ahead by just ordering a new dryer and not paying for my service call."

"How much does a new dryer cost compared to a service call?"

Oscar chuckled and, in his Swedish-accented English, said, "A dryer is about seven hundred dollars, compared to seventy-five dollars for me to show up at your house with tools." He paused, then added, "Is your washer the same vintage? If it is, you're living on borrowed time. I've got a sale going and could sell you a new set for a thousand dollars."

Leaning back and closing my eyes, I tried to envision our savings account balance, then how long it would take us to have enough to pay for either a dryer, or a washer and dryer combo.

"The manufacturer has a promotion going. If you buy the pair, you can pay them off with no interest over the next twelve months."

Resigned to accepting the deal, I asked, "Does the price include hauling away the old appliances?"

"Oh, yah. You betcha," he replied, sounding like a character right out of the movie *Fargo*. "You get delivery, hook up, disposal of the old appliances, and a ninety-day parts and labor warranty."

Sighing, I agreed to the deal. "When can you deliver the new ones?"

"I can do it this afternoon. If you're like most folks who don't lock their houses, I can install them without you using vacation time."

"Do I need to stop in the shop to sign the papers?"

Oscar chuckled. "Are you going to make the payments?"

"Certainly!"

"Peter, I know and trust you. Stop by the showroom when you get a chance. I'll have the loan agreement on my desk."

Still saddened by the thought of buying a new washer and dryer, I went down to get a cup of coffee. The Whistling Pines dining room was full of people finishing their breakfasts and socializing. I drew a cup of coffee from the urn and walked among the tables, greeting people and listening in on the current rumors.

Lyndon Hjelmberg, a recent addition to Whistling Pines, was sitting with Lee Westfall and Howard Johnson. Waving me over to their table, Howard introduced the new resident. "Peter, have you met Captain Hjelmberg?"

I shook Lyndon's hand and said, "We met when Nancy took him on a tour of the facility."

"Yah, that could be," Lyndon replied in a heavy Norwegian accent. "I met so many people. The names aren't sticking in my head."

"Lyndon worked on the iron ore ships for forty-three years," Howard explained. "He ended his career as the ship's captain on the Mary Helen."

Getting a dreamy look, Lyndon said, "I miss being on the water. On the other hand, I do enjoy getting a hot meal three times a day and not slopping my coffee when the weather gets rough."

"I thought the meals on the big ore boats were notoriously good."

Lyndon pulled out a handkerchief and dabbed at his nose. "It depends on the cook.

Sometimes, we ate well. Other times, we got someone who wasn't as good, and we ate sandwiches and soup for the whole trip. The cooks here are darned fine."

Howard changed the topic and asked, "Has anyone opened the puzzle box?"

"Not yet," I replied. "Do you want to give it another try?"

"I don't have the patience," Howard replied. "You need a teenager who's good at doing those Rubik's Cube things to open it."

"I'll keep that in mind," I replied before walking out of the dining room.

I found Jenny in the nurse's office. "We're getting a new washer and dryer."

Her eyes went wide. "I thought you were going to have the dryer repaired?"

"Oscar Halvorson convinced me that the dryer electronics weren't repairable. Since the washer is the same age, it's probably on its last legs, too. He had a no-interest deal on the pair."

Jenny hung her head. "So much for taking a vacation this year."

"Look on the bright side—we won't have to replace all of our underwear."

"Peter, that's not much of an upside," she replied.

In my office, I entered my computer password and searched for colorblind information. Google said, "Red/green color deficiency is the most common type of color blindness. People afflicted with it can't discern between shades of red and green.

Blue/yellow colorblindness is less common. People afflicted with it can't differentiate between blue, yellow, and green."

Further searching revealed that 8% of men and 0.5% of women are colorblind. Of that group, only one in twenty colorblind people have blue/yellow colorblindness. I leaned back and considered the information. Color blindness was much more common than I realized. Although blue/yellow/green color blindness was less common, it wasn't as rare as I would have expected. *I suppose it's possible that the person who swapped out the gas cylinders was colorblind and wouldn't have known he was swapping a blue tank for a green one.*

A second thought struck me. Who, other than a dentist or anesthesiologist, would have ready access to a cylinder of nitrous oxide? The answer that came to mind was obvious – someone who intends to kill off a person reliant on her oxygen supply.

A new search revealed that it is illegal to sell nitrous oxide for recreational purposes. The most common non-anesthesia use of nitrous oxide is in aerosol cans of whipped cream. *The blue cylinder at the church was a lot bigger than an aerosol can of whipped cream.*

Without a knock, my office door swung open. I turned as Brian Johnson sat in my guest chair. "What's the smartest insect?"

Unable to discern how Brian was going to tie a tuba into this joke, I shrugged.

"A spelling bee!" Brian pointed at the Post-it notepad on my desk. "Write that one down for your son."

"I was expecting a tuba somewhere in the punchline," I said as I made a note of Brian's joke.

"I don't have many more tuba jokes that are suitable for mixed audiences. MaryBeth has threatened to beat me if I tell most of them in public."

"Do you screen them on your wife before telling them?"

Brian paused. "She thinks *I* should be able to filter the bad jokes without inflicting them on her."

"How is that going for you?"

"Not very well. I focus on the funny part and not as much on whether it will offend my audience."

"Give me an example."

Brian thought for a moment, then broke into a smile. "What do you call a tuba player who isn't part of a polka band?" When I didn't answer, he told me the punchline, "Unemployed."

"That's not too adult-themed."

"Good! I'll add it to the 'approved' list." He paused, then said, "What instrument does a gynecologist play? A fallopian tuba."

Cringing, I said, "Put that one into the unapproved pile."

"I'll quit now. The rest are even more questionable."

"Really? Do you have many more?"

Ignoring the question, Brian asked, "Can I see your puzzle box?"

After unlocking the bottom drawer of my desk, I removed the puzzle box and handed it to Brian. He slid the few end panels I already knew would move, then shrugged. "I don't have the patience to work this out." He handed the box back to me and said, "I may know what's inside the box."

"I'm relatively certain it's not a tuba," I replied.

"That's obvious. I think it's a treasure map."

"What would that treasure map lead to?"

Brian frowned and replied, "Treasure."

"I was hoping for something more specific."

"Astrid's husband was an antique dealer. It was rumored that he was shady and paid a few cents on the dollar for some items that were very valuable."

"It seems like everyone thinks their family members have a missing Van Gogh or Picasso. In reality, most of those items are much less valuable than the family believes."

"Like I said, one of the rumors is that there's a treasure map in the box."

"One of the rumors? What are the others?"

"Someone said Astrid was extremely frugal and she stashed cash in the box."

I shook the box. "It sounds like the contents may be paper, or something wrapped in paper."

"There you go! There's either a treasure map or cash in the box." Brian stood and took a step toward the door.

"We think Astrid was murdered."

Brian froze. "I thought she just tipped over and died. I heard that there were thirty people there who saw it happen. She wasn't shot, stabbed, or bludgeoned. How could that be murder?"

"Someone swapped out her oxygen bottle for nitrous oxide, and she was asphyxiated."

Brian blinked twice, obviously stumped by the information. "Where would someone get a cylinder of laughing gas?"

"You know that nitrous oxide is laughing gas?"

"I was a chemist in my previous life. I know all kinds of useless things." He paused, then smiled, "Including a lexicon of tuba jokes."

"Where would someone get a cylinder of nitrous oxide? You can't just walk into a store and buy one."

"I'd break into a dentist's office. That's the only place I've ever heard of someone using laughing gas. I guess it relaxes people, in addition to making them giddy."

Leaning back and staring at the ceiling after Brian's departure, I thought, *Where would someone get nitrous oxide? Would a dentist report a missing nitrous oxide cylinder? Would a dentist office miss a stolen nitrous oxide cylinder?*

Sherry interrupted my thoughts. "I've got a problem."

"How can I help?" I asked.

"My dad was interrogating me about my duties here, and he has a problem with the lack of structure."

Dumbfounded, I must've waited too long to respond.

"There are some planned activities, like the regular movies and shopping trips. But a lot of what you have me do is spur-of-the-moment and unplanned. He thinks I should press you to make the activities more...planned."

"I agree with your father. However, the residents like variety. They want their meals served on time, but they like different things on the menu every week. They like movie day, but they don't want a mystery or comedy every week. I mix things up to provide them with something that keeps them interested and asking about what's upcoming."

"I heard that SeaWorld trainers have to change their training routines because the dolphins get bored with the same things all the time," Sherry added.

"I'd like to believe our residents are smarter than dolphins. But the same principle applies to our schedule. Take you, for example. They love you." I grinned.

"What's that got to do with changing the schedule?"

"You're a fresh face with enthusiasm and new ideas. They love having you here, and they love interacting with you."

Sherry's smile faded. "Hulda Packer seems less enthusiastic about my presence."

"Hulda is an unhappy woman. She likes to find the bad in everything. However, she shows up for your programs, which means she likes the things you're doing. And, by extension, she likes you. You've added a spark to our programs."

"I'll tell Dad that."

"What else does he say about your job?"

"I think he's torn about it. He's pleased that I'm employed. He was sure I'd be living with them forever while trying to find a job as an artist. And, he agrees this is better than waiting tables and cleaning hotel rooms. On the other hand, I think he'd hoped I would see the light and consider something more pious."

"Does he want you to attend the seminary?"

Sherry snorted. "God, no. Oops. Sorry. I shouldn't take the Lord's name in vain."

"Why doesn't he want you to attend the seminary? I thought every preacher wanted their kids to follow in their footsteps."

"Peter, there are no female Svenska Gotter ministers. He'd be happy if I married a minister but me attending a seminary would be unacceptable." Sherry paused. "Speaking of marrying a minister, that's one of the other things he doesn't like about me working here. There aren't any prospective unmarried young men on the staff."

Grinning, I replied, "I can't help you with that issue."

"I went on a date with Chip Rindahl, who manages the bowling alley. Dad wasn't pleased about that, either. He thinks I should set my sights higher."

"Don't try too hard. Sometimes, love just happens."

Sherry stood and said, "How did you get so smart?"

"I've had a lot of life lessons. A person learns a lot from failures and frustrations." I paused, then remembered a quote. "Experience is a cruel teacher. You don't get the lessons until after the tests."

"I don't get it."

"Like your modeling career. You thought it was going to be fun and rewarding. You didn't get the lesson about the Svenska Gotter protest until after you'd been a model. The lesson came after the experience."

"Huh. I never thought of it in those terms."

"A lot of life lessons come with bruises. Cherish them and learn."

Chapter 5

After stopping at Oscar's Appliance to sign the loan agreement on the new washer and dryer, I drove to the Methodist/Presbyterian Church, hoping to find someone who might've witnessed the oxygen bottle swap and Astrid's collapse. Two cars were in the parking lot and the main doors were unlocked. I was drawn to the sound of the vacuum cleaner. I startled a man who appeared to be well past retirement age when I walked in through a side door and tapped his shoulder.

"Jeez!" he exclaimed, clutching the front of his plaid shirt.

"I'm sorry," I said, raising my voice to be heard over the vacuum cleaner, "I was hoping to speak with someone who'd been in church the day that Astrid Tostenrud died."

Recovering from his surprise, the man switched off the vacuum. "Pastor Evans is in his office." He gestured toward a closed office door at the end of a hallway lined with classrooms.

"Were you here that morning?"

The man considered the question as if it was more than a yes or no answer. "It depends," he replied.

"Depends on what?" I asked.

"Well, I was in the church, and I saw Astrid on the floor when the firemen arrived. However, I wasn't sitting with the congregation during the service."

"I don't understand."

"I was making coffee to be served after the service."

"Ah," I replied. "You don't know who swapped Astrid's oxygen tank?"

"I didn't know her oxygen had been exchanged. I think you'd better talk to Pastor Evans."

At the end of the hallway, I knocked on a door with a brass nameplate that read, *Robert Evans – Pastor*. A voice from inside invited me in as the vacuum cleaner started up.

Pastor Evans was a heavyset man with a fuzzy mop of white hair. He was dressed casually, unlike most of the other pastors in Two Harbors, who typically wore a suit or sport coat." I'm Bob Evans," he said as he stood and stepped from behind a beautiful wood desk. It was so tidy I found it hard to believe it wasn't staged.

Shaking his hand, I said, "I'm Peter Rogers, the recreation director from Whistling Pines."

"I've seen you driving their van around town." He gestured for me to sit in a guest chair. "You provide a wonderful ministry for your residents. I see them shopping in town and attending events."

I'd never considered my job a ministry, so I was somewhat unsure how to respond. "I like to offer activities that enrich the residents' lives."

Sitting behind his desk, the pastor leaned on his elbows and smiled. "The variety of your offerings is a statement to your creativity. I'd never come up with a painting class that used nude models."

"Well, that evolution of the art class was unplanned."

The pastor chuckled. "I'd guessed it was something ad-lib by the art instructor. I don't imagine that you chose to have the Svenska Gotters protest."

"That was never a part of the plan," I replied. Changing the topic, I asked, "What can you tell me about the day Astrid Tostenrud died?"

The smile melted from Pastor Evans' face, and he leaned back. "That was terrible. I don't know what I could tell you."

"I watched the video replay of that service, posted on your website. It appears that someone helps Astrid change her oxygen tank before the service. Do you know who that was?"

"Why are you inquiring?"

"It's a rather long story. Astrid bequeathed her piano to Whistling Pines. In the course of tuning, we found an item inside the piano. In the process of trying to find Astrid's family, I was told that her death may not have been entirely natural."

The pastor was surprised by that information. "If that's the case, I'd expect you to speak with the police."

"The police chief sometimes asks me to ask some discreet questions before stirring things up by opening a full investigation."

Frowning, the pastor said, "I'm still not sure what your role is."

"It's hard to explain," I replied. "Officially, I'm a reserve officer with the Two Harbors Police Department. Unofficially, I'm the liaison between Whistling Pines and the City. I've assisted Kerry with a few investigations when he's busy or short of resources."

"I remember something about you and the fire chief on a stakeout after the bait shop burned down."

"That wasn't our finest hour."

"You caught the arsonist. I'd say you were successful." Evans paused, then added, "And weren't you the one who caught the person who poisoned the baker?"

Sighing, I nodded. "Even a blind squirrel finds an acorn now and then."

"Why are you interested in Astrid's oxygen tank? I thought she just got short of breath and died from her COPD."

"On the video, I can see someone swapping out the oxygen tank before the service began."

Evans nodded. "Astrid was getting short of breath. As I recall, someone checked, and her oxygen tank was empty."

"Do you recall who swapped that cylinder for her?"

"Sure, that was Dr. Robertson, Astrid's nephew."

Hiding my surprise that Astrid's nephew may have supplied the nitrous oxide cylinder that killed her, I said, "I don't recall a doctor named Robertson in town."

"Clifford Robertson is a dentist with a DDS, rather than a medical doctor with an MD. He had a spare oxygen tank in his car. He swapped it and we went on with the service."

"I'd like to speak with him. Where is his office located?"

"He retired several years ago and closed his Two Harbors office. I heard that Beaver Bay persuaded him to open an office there where he works part-time." The pastor paused. "I think Doc was bored after he retired, so it was a win-win when the town offered to lease him a closed store front so he can work a couple of days a week."

Thinking about the small town of Beaver Bay, which was hardly more than a bar, a few shops, and a strip mall on the highway to Silver Bay, I asked, "Does he live here, or in Beaver Bay?"

"He lives in one of the big houses overlooking Lake Superior. I think his address is on Slater Drive." Frowning again, the pastor asked, "You don't think Doc was involved in Astrid's death, do you?"

"I imagine there was some confusion that morning and there might have been a tragic accident."

"Astrid seemed to be okay. As a matter of fact, her rendition of "Onward, Christian Soldiers" was rather rousing. She seemed to be quite enthused and happy. Well, right up until she tipped over."

I thanked Pastor Bob for his time and left his office wondering where to go with the information about Dr. Robertson. The custodian had completed his vacuuming and was nowhere in sight when I left the building. Walking to my car, I considered passing the dentist information over to Kerry. That thought was interrupted when my cell phone rang.

Fumbling the phone while pulling it from my pocket, I was too distracted to process the THFD caller ID when I answered the call on the third, and possibly final ring. "This is Peter."

Filled with desperation, the male voice said, "Doc, you've got to help."

After a second, I connected the caller ID with Sparky's voice. "What's wrong?"

"Everything! My mom and Wendy are both on the warpath. I'm afraid to go home or to Mom's house."

"Where are you?"

"I'm hiding at the fire station."

"The fire station hardly seems like a hiding place."

"Aw, crap. You're probably right. It's the first place Wendy will look for me, isn't it."

"What is the problem?"

"Mom is still convinced that Wendy poisoned her. Wendy is mad because Mom is mad at her. It's a lose-lose situation. What should I do?"

"I'll ask a question that will make your pathway clear: Which one are you living with?"

"How does that clear up anything?"

I leaned against the side of my car and pinched the bridge of my nose. "It's simple, Sparky. Wendy is having your kid and you're living together. You have to keep her happy."

"It's easier to keep Mom happy. All I'd have to do is move home and cancel the wedding."

"Is that what you want to do?"

"Not really."

"Sometimes the easy path isn't the best path. Figure out how to make peace with Wendy. You don't *have to* live with your mother. As a matter of fact, at some point, you were going to move away from home. Now is the time to cut your apron strings."

"I've never worn an apron."

"That's a metaphor for going off on your own. You are cutting the apron strings that bind you to your mother."

"But I like my mother."

"You're moving on to the next phase of your life and that involves a wife and child."

"Could you come by the fire station and explain that a little better?"

After checking my watch, I said, "I'll be there in ten minutes."

* * *

There were three cars in the fire station parking lot when I arrived. The building's side door was ajar, with a trickle of water running onto the sidewalk. Without considering that, I walked into a mist of water, then into a stream that hit me in the face.

"Oh, shit. I'm so sorry," Stella Hygge said as she turned the garden hose away from me, directing it onto the soapy side of the fire truck she was washing. Rushing to the spigot, she shut off the water and returned carrying towels. "Here," she said, handing me a towel.

I stepped back as she started to pat my pants legs dry. "I've got it, Stella."

"Sorry. I was going to quit before I got to your crotch," she said with a devilish smile.

"I'm relieved by that statement," I said as I stripped off my sodden jacket, then wiped my hair with the towel.

Hearing my voice, Sparky rushed out of the office. "I'm so glad you're here."

"You could've warned Stella that I was coming," I said as I blotted my pants."

"It never occurred to me," Sparky replied. "Why did you squirt Peter with the hose?"

"He startled me." She shrugged, then added, "It's less lethal than shooting him."

"You would've shot me?" I asked.

"Well, not here. But if you'd broken into my house, I would've peppered your hide with #9 birdshot."

Sparky nodded. "That's a pretty good deterrent when it comes to confronting a burglar."

"What do you want to discuss, Sparky?"

He paused, staring at Stella. "I think it'd be better if we spoke in the privacy of the office."

"Are you kidding?" Stella asked. "You've been whining to me for an hour about being caught between your fiancée and your mother. Now you want to consult Peter without my input?"

"Peter's advice might involve sexual situations I wouldn't be comfortable discussing in front of you."

"Sparky, I can assure you that nothing I suggest will involve sex or anything sexual."

Stella's smile got wider. "Dang. I was hoping for relationship advice. If sex is off the table, I might not be interested."

Sparky's blush was comical. "I can't discuss relationships with anyone here, at the fire station. The conversation always degenerates into something dirty or disgusting."

Trying to look offended, Stella put her hand on her chest. "I would never engage in disgusting or dirty talk. Never!"

"You were the one who asked if Mom and I were sharing a bed."

"I was just asking for perspective, you know, to help understand your mommy issues."

"All right," I said, trying not to smile. "Sparky's issues are serious, and they need serious answers."

"Thank you, Peter," Sparky said as he glared at Stella. "Women are so..."

"We're what, Sparky? Go on, spit it out."

"Overly emotional."

"I may be unpredictable and a bit foul-mouthed, but I'm *not* overly emotional."

"How old are you, Stella?" I asked.

"A gentleman never asks a lady's age," she said, then replied, "twenty-nine."

"You've dealt with relationship issues and break-ups, right?" I asked.

"Sure. I've had my heart broken."

"You should be able to relate to Sparky's issue."

"Like hell I can! I moved away from home when I was eighteen and lived in an apartment with four other women. I've never had *mommy issues*. I've lived on my own for years and my mother treats me as an independent adult."

"Look at it from Wendy's perspective," I suggested.

"From the *harlot's* point of view?" she asked.

Sparky's look of surprise was priceless. "I told you about the harlot thing in confidence! You weren't supposed to mention it to anyone."

Stella's eyes sparkled. "Did I say harlot out loud? I'm sorry. It just slipped out."

"See! This is why I wanted to talk to you in the office instead of in front of Stella. She's a blabbermouth."

"I've never said a word about you having sex with the harlot in the back of the fire truck."

"See!" Sparky complained. "That's a secret. You promised never to tell anyone about that."

"Sparky," I said softly, trying to defuse the escalation. "I didn't hear about you and Wendy having sex in the fire truck from Stella."

"Who told you?"

"You told me, and Wendy told Jenny, who also told me."

"Jeez! Does the whole town know?"

Stella nodded. "Probably. It's a small town."

"Let's get back to Sparky's problem," I suggested. "Stella, pretend you're Wendy and help Sparky find the right words to bring peace."

"Okay, I'm the pregnant harlot. What are you planning to say to me, so I don't kill you in your sleep?"

Looking terrorized, Sparky said, "You'd kill me in my sleep?"

"I would if I found out you'd taken your mother's side over me in an argument."

"That's it! I'm moving back in with Mom. She won't kill me in my sleep."

"That's just a figure of speech," I said. "Wendy won't kill you in your sleep."

"Nah," Stella agreed. "She'll probably just cut off your 'man parts.'"

"Stop that, Stella." I looked at Sparky. "Wendy won't do that either. But you need to patch things up with her. You can't move back with your mother."

"Fine. I'll sleep on the couch in the fire station."

Taking pity on Sparky, Stella said, "Let's start over. I'll be Wendy. What are you going to say to her?"

"I'm sorry my mother hates you because you poisoned her. What can I do to make it up to you?"

Grimacing, I said, "Sparky, it'd be better if you didn't take your mother's side on the food poisoning thing. Try something like, 'Wendy, I'm with you. Let's move past my mother's accusations and talk about wedding plans.'"

"I need to address the food poisoning thing."

I glared at Stella, who appeared ready to throw out a witty reply. "No, you don't need to address the food poisoning thing. Whatever happened was NOT caused by

Wendy. Jenny said that quite clearly. If there had been something wrong with that meal, both you and Wendy would have been sick, too. Whatever made your mother ill was something she'd eaten at least a day earlier."

Sparky drew a breath and took Stella's hand. "Wendy, I'm sorry I took Mom's side. You're not to blame for what made her sick. Let's move on."

I turned to Stella. "How would Wendy reply?"

"Oh, Sparky, thank you for coming to your senses. Let's move to Minneapolis so we're farther from your mother."

Sparky had never considered the possibility that Wendy might want to move and was at a loss for words. "Sparky," I said, "Wendy probably won't say that. She will want you to take her side on this."

Nodding, Stella added, "And on every issue that forces you to make a choice on which side to take."

"Is that true, Doc?"

"As soon as you say, 'I do,' you and Wendy are together through all the situations covered in your vows, as well as any other that arise."

"Yeah," Stella added. "There's an unspoken vow in there that covers 'all other situations not covered by what's been said.'"

I nodded. "The Navy calls that 'other duties as assigned.'"

With his mouth falling open, Sparky considered the enormity of what we'd said. "Other duties as assigned?"

"Yep," Stella replied as I nodded.

"This marriage thing is huge."

"It is," I agreed, "as are fathering a child and being a parent."

"Kind of makes you rethink your moments of ecstasy in the back of the fire truck, huh?" Stella said, smiling.

"Why didn't someone warn me?"

Closing my eyes and biting my bottom lip, I paused. "Haven't you noticed how your friends changed when they got married and had children?"

"Why do you think I'm still single?" Stella asked. "I haven't found a guy I can trust to fulfill those wedding vows in the way I expect." She paused. "Well, that and finding a guy who makes my heart skip a beat when he walks into the room."

I put my arm around Sparky's shoulder before he could think about Stella's comments too carefully. "Go home. Tell Wendy you love her. Promise you'll take her side when it comes to a decision about her versus your mother."

As Sparky walked out the door Stella yelled, "A nice bouquet of flowers buys you a lot of Brownie points!"

I watched Sparky get into his car still looking shell-shocked. Hoping he'd come up with the correct words when he got home, I walked back into the firehouse.

Stella was rinsing the soapy residue off the truck. Trying not to startle her again, I walked to the spigot and turned off the water. After a moment of confusion, she turned to me. "You're still here?"

"Tell me about the rescue call to the Methodist/Presbyterian Church."

"The one where the old woman died?"

"Yeah. Tell me what happened."

After recapping the call and the trip from the firehouse to the church, Stella explained how they'd started CPR and put an oxygen mask on Astrid.

"She was hooked up to a bottle of gas when you arrived, right?"

"Yeah, we took the cannula from under her nose and put a mask over her face. Karl did CPR and I squeezed the bag to pump oxygen into her lungs."

"Did you notice anything unusual about Astrid's oxygen bottle?"

Stella thought for a second, while frowning. "Not really?"

"Was it green or blue?"

"Oxygen bottles are always green," she replied.

"Are you certain that Stella's gas bottle was green?"

"I was focused on the patient, not the color of the bottle in her cart."

"Is there a computer with internet access in the office?"

"Sure," she said, leading me to an office as cluttered as I expected Sparky's office to be. After booting up the computer, Stella asked, "What do you want me to look up?"

"Pull up the church's website and click on the service the day of your call." When the video started to play, I told her to focus on Astrid and her gas cylinder. After a bit, we saw the dentist leave and return with a replacement gas cylinder. "Stop there."

"Okay," Stella said. "What am I looking for?"

"What color is the replacement gas cylinder?"

She toggled the video backward and forward several times, then leaned back. "That's not oxygen."

"No, it's nitrous oxide."

"That's laughing gas."

"I think Astrid was asphyxiated with nitrous oxide."

After digesting that news, Stella shook her head. "No one else got sick."

"No one else was breathing a stream of it being shot into their nose."

"Well, shit."

"Do you remember what happened to her blue gas cylinder after you arrived?"

"No one came near us while we were doing CPR. After the ambulance took her away, I packed up our gear and carried it back to the truck."

"Do you recall anyone removing the gas cylinder?"

"I don't think so." Stella paused. "Wait. There was an old guy who was fooling around with something by the organ. I remember because he backed into me and excused himself.”

“Was it Doctor Robertson, the dentist?”

“I don’t know who it was. No, wait. I think it was someone dressed just like the guy who brought the replacement cylinder into the church.”

“Would you recognize him?” I asked.

“I doubt it. Like I said, he just excused himself and walked away. I just remember he was as old as the other parishioners and was nicely dressed. Not many people dress up for church anymore.”

Chapter 6

I'd just driven out of the church parking lot when my cell phone rang. Pulling to the curb as I wrestled the phone free from a pocket covered by my seatbelt, I answered before it rolled over to voicemail. "Peter, this is Alison at the front desk. There's a man here to see you about a box."

Frowning, I asked, "Is he a resident?"

"No, he said he's a locksmith."

I tipped my head back and sighed. I'd totally forgotten that Ray Gradien said he'd stop and attempt to unlock the puzzle box. "Is Wendy nearby?"

"I haven't seen her for a while."

"Are any members of the staff within sight?"

"No, but Nancy is in her office."

"Please tell Nancy I'm on my way back, then ask if she'll retrieve the puzzle box from the bottom drawer of my desk and show it to the locksmith. I should be there in ten minutes."

"Okay," the young receptionist replied.

Pulling back onto the road, I felt stupid for having forgotten about the locksmith commitment. There were too many things going on, and I was losing control. The whole discussion with Sparky and Stella had taken my mind places it didn't need to go and diverted me from important things, like my job.

After parking my car, I jogged to the Whistling Pines front door. Looking up from her computer, Alison pointed toward the dining room. "The locksmith is talking to Mrs. Packer," she said.

A slender gray-haired man was sitting at a table near the dining room entrance. He was holding a coffee mug and Hulda Packer, gesturing with her finger extended, appeared to be lecturing him. The puzzle box sat on the table between them. I pulled out a chair and sat down next to the locksmith. "Mr. Gradien, I'm Peter Rogers. I apologize for not being here to meet you."

The man's smile was friendly and reassuring, possibly because I'd interrupted Hulda's lecture. "We hadn't really set a time to meet. I got through my job at the house and drove over without contacting you."

"I see Nancy found the box for you."

Ray nodded to Hulda and said, "Yes, Mrs. Packer and I were discussing my time in her classroom."

The locksmith appeared to be about sixty, which meant he'd been one of Hulda's students more than half a century ago. "Do you remember him, Hulda?" I asked.

"Pfft," Hulda replied. "I had a thousand students over the years. I only remember the very best and the stinkers."

"But I remember Mrs. Packer," Ray replied. "It's hard to forget the person who rapped your knuckles with a wooden ruler once a day."

Hulda straightened in her chair. "I enforced discipline and respect in my classes."

"Or terror," Ray replied.

"Did you look at my box?" I asked.

"I opened it."

I picked up the box, which looked the same as when I'd put it into the drawer. "It appears to be as I left it."

Hulda sniffled. "He was sitting here with it open. All those little slats were sticking out. It was a mess. I made it neat."

Trying hard not to express my frustration, I handed the box back to Ray. "Would you open it again, please."

Ray turned the box end for end, then started sliding the hidden panels. "I don't exactly recall how I opened it. Mrs. Packer distracted me when she put it back together. Since then, we have talked about school days."

"Do you remember what was inside?" I asked. "Did it contain money?"

"No." Ray replied as he turned the box and slid the little panels, trying to recreate the series of moves he'd made earlier. "There were papers inside, but not any money."

"Did you look at the papers?" I asked.

"I didn't read them if that's what you're asking," Ray replied as he continued to manipulate the panels, at times reversing moves he'd previously made.

"I think it was a deed," Hulda suggested. "It looked like it had a seal on it, like they'd put on in the county office. Or maybe a birth certificate."

"Is that what you saw, Ray?"

Frowning as he studied the box, Ray shook his head. "I didn't see any seal. I think it was just someone's chicken scratching. The handwriting was terrible."

"There was a handwritten note inside? What did it say?"

"Like I said, Hulda took the box and closed it before I got more than a glimpse of the contents." With the lid slightly ajar, Ray handed the box back to me. "This is as far as I can get. I bet you could shine a flashlight through the crack and maybe make out some of the writing."

"You can't remember how to get it fully open?" I asked.

"Not really. I just fiddled with it and at one point the top slid completely open. That's when Mrs. Packer showed up."

I carried the box to the front desk and interrupted a conversation Alison was having with a resident who couldn't unlock her mailbox. "Let me borrow the emergency flashlight for a moment."

"There's an emergency flashlight?" Alison replied.

"In the bottom left cabinet, there's a roster for checking headcount after an evacuation and a flashlight."

Alison handed me the flashlight, and I focused the beam on the open crack. I could see the folded edge of a sheet of paper, but nothing was visible except for a few letters of handwriting and a bit of a drawing.

"Thanks," I said before carrying the puzzle box back where Hulda was lecturing Ray on his grammar. I handed the box back to Ray as I sat. "I can see the edge of a note, but I can't read anything."

Ray considered the slight opening he'd created after the last set of slides. "I've got a big screwdriver in the truck," he said. "I could pry it open, but that would ruin that beautiful box."

Shaking my head, I accepted the box back from him. "That'll be my last resort. Thanks."

Ray and I stood. Hulda was unusually quiet as I thanked Ray and shook his hand. I was about to leave when Hulda stopped me. "Astrid's husband was in the war."

"I'd heard that he was in the Korean War."

Flipping her fingers like I was distracting her with an immaterial and trivial fact, she said, "I heard he'd shipped some things home before he left Korea."

"I think a lot of soldiers send home mementos and souvenirs."

Receiving the *shut up until I'm through talking* look, I stopped. "Eugene Tostenrud shipped home valuable things. Things he'd stolen from villages that had been ruined and abandoned during the battles."

"I'm pretty sure this box only contains documents, not stolen treasure."

"Maybe it contains a treasure map showing where he buried the stolen things."

Knowing that Hulda wouldn't let go of that bone of contention until she was satisfied, I understood her and was going to act accordingly, I said, "I'll keep the box locked in a safe place until we get it open and examine the contents."

Satisfied, Hulda nodded. I quickly exited and returned to my office, where I locked the box in my bottom desk drawer. Now curious, I searched the internet for information about items stolen or lost during the Korean War. The first search screen popped up, stating that over 182,000 cultural artifacts were stolen or lost from Korea between 1950 and 1953. The US has returned over 8,000 cultural treasures since 2007. Nearly 100,000 items remain unaccounted for. Some were undoubtedly destroyed in battle, but it's thought that thousands are still in the hands of collectors or stored by veterans' families who are unaware of the cultural or monetary value.

I leaned back in my chair and thought, *Astrid's husband was known as a shady antique dealer. It's plausible he sent back, or returned with, culturally valuable items.* I stared at the locked drawer. My cell phone chirped, and I answered it.

"Have you made supper plans?" Jenny asked.

"Nope."

"How would you feel about a Culver's hamburger and fries?"

Surprised by the suggestion of fast food, I hesitated, wondering if it was a trick question. "I'd be happy with that."

"Good. Pick up burgers while I get Amy from daycare."

"I'm on my way."

Chapter 7

I gathered the bags and burger wrappers while Jenny cleaned the ketchup from Amy's fingers and picked up bits of fries, burger bun, and pickle scattered during our daughter's meal. Amy was old enough for finger food, but she seemed more focused on smearing it around than on eating it.

Having carried glasses to the kitchen sink, Jeremy returned to the dining room and watched Jenny sweeping crumbs from the floor. "If we had a dog, he'd eat all those bits and you wouldn't have to pick up Amy's scraps." Jeremy smiled and quirked an eyebrow.

"A dog comes with his own set of pick-up issues," Jenny replied.

"I'd take care of him," Jeremy quickly added, a bit too hopeful.

"Are you through with your homework?" I asked before we got deeper into the dog discussion.

"Mostly. I can do the rest tomorrow morning, before math."

"Finish it now, and I'll check it."

Sighing, Jeremy retrieved his backpack from the corner. "There's really not that much left, and you really don't need to check it."

I put out my hand. "Show me."

Looking pained, Jeremy pulled a worksheet from his backpack and handed it to me. The only thing he'd done was write his name on the top. "This hasn't even been started."

"I started it," he replied. "I just didn't get very far before you came home with supper."

"Find a pencil and start solving the problems," I said, returning the paper to him.

A knock on the back door interrupted our discussion. "Can you get that, Peter?" Jenny called from the living room.

"Sure," I said, walking to the door. On the top step, I found Sparky, literally hat in hand, looking like he'd lost his last friend. "Doc, you've got to help me."

I held the door so he could enter, then asked, "What's wrong?"

"Wendy's on the warpath."

"Can you be more specific?"

Sparky froze, trying to articulate the problem. "Wendy thinks I'm taking my mother's side."

" I'm trying to take care of computer issues, and I keep getting interrupted."

Recalling that Sparky had a *day job* working from home as the Lake County computer resource, I said, "Tell me what's happening."

"Well, it all started when she got home. I was in my office trying to recover the data on the county assessor's crashed computer. Wendy was banging cupboard doors and muttering to herself. I said, 'Hi, honey,' and her face turned red. I asked her what was wrong, and she said, 'you don't even know what's wrong?' I said I didn't. Then she threw her arms up, stormed into the bedroom, and slammed the door."

"Uh oh."

Sparky's eyes went wide. "Uh oh? It's that bad?"

"You've got to figure out why she's mad without asking her about it again."

"How do I do that?"

Placing my hand on Sparky's shoulder, I said, "That's one of life's greatest mysteries."

"Doc, you're not being helpful."

I stepped into the dining room and called out to Jenny, who'd gone upstairs with Amy. "Honey, Sparky's got a problem."

A moment later, Jenny walked downstairs. "What's up?"

"Tell her, Sparky."

"Wendy's mad and I don't know why. Saying that I didn't know why she was angry just made her madder."

"Uh oh. You don't know why she's mad at you?"

Wringing his Two Harbors Fire Department cap in his hands, Sparky said, "I don't have a clue!"

"Think back about everything you did today," Jenny suggested.

"I got a call from the tax assessor about the computer crash, so I drove over to the government center. After I determined there was no easy fix for the problem, I brought the problem laptop home. I was trying to transfer his data to an external hard drive."

"Did Wendy ask you to do something that didn't get done?"

Sparky frowned, deep in thought. "I get kinda focused when I'm into computers." Scratching his head, Sparky said, "I don't remember forgetting anything."

"Ahh," Jenny said. "It appears you forgot to do, or get, whatever it was that Wendy asked you to take care of."

"How am I supposed to correct that when I can't remember whatever it was that I forgot?"

"Did she give you a shopping list?" I asked.

Sparky dug into his pockets, then showed me his empty hands. "I don't think so."

"Were you supposed to pick up dinner on your way home?"

"My mom brought over cabbage rolls. I thought we'd probably have them for supper."

Nodding, Jenny smiled. "How does Wendy feel about your mother's cabbage rolls?"

"I don't remember Wendy having a cabbage roll opinion. This morning she said something about Chinese food sounding good, but her taste seems to change between when she says something like that and when I pick it up."

A sly smile crept onto Jenny's face. "Here's what you're going to do—walk home and apologize. Then, tell Wendy you're taking her out for supper." Jenny put her hand on Sparky's arm and nudged him toward the door. "Let her choose the restaurant."

Pausing at the door, Sparky asked, "What am I apologizing for?"

"It doesn't make any difference," I said. "Just say you're sorry and that you're taking her out for supper."

Nodding, Sparky stepped outside. "Is this going to happen often after we're married?"

"Probably," I replied. "Eventually, you'll be able to read the cues and apologize before she erupts."

"Read which cues?"

"You'll figure them out," I replied, closing the door to end the discussion.

Jenny started laughing. "Have I ever done that to you?"

"Not lately."

"I used to?" she asked.

"Mostly when you were pregnant. Your mood swings were sometimes tough to read."

Cocking her head, Jenny asked, "Did you ever apologize without knowing what you'd done wrong?"

I was saved from answering the question when Jeremy yelled, "Dad, I'm stuck on a word problem."

Jeremy and I were reasoning through the word problem when I heard voices outside, followed by the sound of Sparky's pickup starting. Jenny called from the living room, "I heard the pickup and no gunshots. Sparky's apology must've worked."

"Let's hope Sparky and Wendy's relationship issues aren't something we have to deal with every night."

"Why did the chief apologize?" Jeremy asked.

"We'll probably never know."

* * *

Amy was in bed, and Jenny was reading to Jeremy when I heard a car pull into our driveway. I met Kerry Stone at the back door just before he knocked. "Did Wendy kill Sparky?" I asked.

Looking confused, Kerry asked, "What are you talking about?"

I gestured for Kerry to enter, then explained our discussion with Sparky.

"I need you to go back to Whistling Pines with me. Someone broke into your office."

"You're kidding," I said.

Shaking his head, Kerry replied, "It appears that you're either really messy, or someone vandalized your office."

Taking a hoodie from a peg by the door I asked, "Am I driving myself or am I riding with you?"

"Ride with me. You can explain what's going on with your time capsule."

"It's a puzzle box, not a time capsule," I explained as we walked to Kerry's unmarked cruiser.

"You found it inside a donated piano, right?"

"Yes. It belonged to Astrid Tostenrud."

"What did you find inside the box?" Kerry asked as he drove toward Whistling Pines.

"I haven't been able to open it." I paused, then added, "Actually, the locksmith opened it, but Hulda Packer thought it was messy, so she closed it again."

"What was inside it?"

"Um, it's complicated."

"What's inside was complicated?"

"Ray Gradien and Hulda didn't actually examine the contents before closing it."

"Didn't exactly examine the contents? What does that mean?"

"They saw papers inside, but Ray didn't read them."

"Bottom line, you still don't know what's inside the box?"

"Not entirely. I know there are papers inside. Oh, and there's handwriting on the paper."

Kerry glanced at me. "Really? There was writing on the paper? What a novel concept."

"I don't need your sarcasm. Oscar Wilde said sarcasm is the lowest form of wit."

"There's more to that quote," Kerry said as we pulled into the Whistling Pines parking lot. "Sarcasm is the lowest form of wit, but the highest form of intelligence."

"When did you take an English class?" I asked.

"It may come as a surprise to you, but most senior Army officers have college degrees and are well-read."

"Huh," I replied as I stepped out of the car. "You could've fooled me."

"Listen, sailor. The Army is full of professionals."

"The Marines had a saying, 'The only difference between the Army and the Boy Scouts is that the Scouts have adult leaders.'"

Kerry faked a laugh. "That's a good one."

Hulda stopped us near the dining room entrance. "Who called the cops?"

Touching Hulda's shoulder, Kerry smiled. "It's okay, Mrs. Packer. The situation is under control."

Huffing, Hulda pushed her walker away. "I find that hard to believe. The situation here is never under control."

We walked to my office in silence. The door was ajar, and the wood splintered around the knob, suggesting someone had used a screwdriver to pry the door open. Inside, there were papers strewn around, apparently pulled from the now-open desk drawers.

"What's missing?" Kerry asked.

I looked at him incredulously. "I can't tell what's here. So, there's no way to know what's missing." The words were barely out of my mouth when I was struck by the obvious answer. "Someone was looking for the puzzle box."

"So, it's missing," he replied.

"I put it into the trunk of my car after I met with the locksmith."

"The trunk of your car?"

"Hulda mentioned that Astrid Tostenrud's husband had been in Korea and had shipped mementos home after the war."

"Do you think there's some kind of treasure inside the box?" Kerry asked.

"I saw a handwritten note inside. I suspect Eugene Tostenrud may have explained where he stashed items he'd 'liberated' from Korea during the war. I felt uneasy about leaving the box in my office."

"But you locked your office. You never lock that door."

"It seemed like the thing to do after several people saw us handling the puzzle box today. You know, just to make people think the box was stored here."

"That ruse apparently worked. I assume someone was looking for the box." Kerry paused as if a thought was forming. "It's really too bad you didn't see what was inside the box. That might've identified the vandal and Astrid's murderer."

"We'll get the box open again," I said, trying to sound confident.

"Luckily, there's no statute of limitations on charging a murderer."

"Yeah, yeah. I'll get it open soon." Looking at the office mess, I thought about how long the clean up and sorting would take. "I assume you'll cordon off this crime scene until after the Bureau of Criminal Apprehension techs dust it for prints."

"I wasn't planning to call the BCA about this."

"The murderer might be the person who broke in."

"Or Hulda might've been unwilling to wait until tomorrow to find out which movie you were showing on Thursday."

"That's posted on the bulletin board."

Smiling with the unscarred side of his face, Kerry said, "You really struggle with sarcasm, don't you?"

"It's not something I deal with on a regular basis. Is it a regular *cop* thing?"

Kerry gestured for me to follow him down the hallway. "Sarcasm is one of the ways cops stay sane. It's a way of venting without screaming in frustration."

"Do you often want to scream in frustration?" I asked.

"Only every time I deal with some dumb criminal or civilian."

"Is that a daily thing?"

Kerry pushed open the front door. "Sometimes, it's an hourly thing. Just this afternoon, I had someone come in to report that his car had been stolen from the grocery store parking lot."

"That frustrated you?"

"What frustrated me was that he'd left the car running. The battery was weak, and he was afraid that if he turned the engine off, it might not start again."

"That seems reasonable," I replied, trying to sound sincere.

"Don't start with me, Rogers. I know you're smart enough to know how stupid that was."

I climbed into Kerry's cruiser and fastened the seatbelt. "There's a great quote from John Cleese about people needing to be reasonably smart to realize how stupid they are."

"Sadly, there's a lot of truth in that quote."

"What's your plan?" I asked.

"Relative to Astrid's alleged murder?"

"I think it's more than alleged."

"True. She is dead, so that's not an allegation. On the other hand, we don't have any sign of malice to indicate she was murdered. Her death could've been a tragic accident." Kerry paused, then added, "I thought you were going to speak to the dentist."

Turning toward Kerry, I said, "You do understand that I'm not a trained forensic interviewer like you."

"That's why you're perfect for this interview. The dentist won't suspect you're collecting evidence that might be used at his trial."

"Isn't there some Supreme Court decision about questioning someone without a Miranda warning?"

"The Miranda warning isn't read until the person is arrested. Besides, you're not a law enforcement officer. You'll just be having a discussion."

"Right. I walk in and say something like, 'Hi! I'm here to discuss the murder I think you committed. Why did you do it?'"

"You'll be more subtle, but that's what you need to accomplish."

"No."

Kerry waited for a moment, then turned toward me. "No, what?"

"No, I'm not interviewing murderers."

"They're suspects, not murderers."

"I don't care if you only suspect they're murderers. The dentist *might be* a murderer. I'm not interviewing him or any of the other suspects."

"Fine. I'll have Sparky talk to the dentist."

I glared at Kerry. "Are you crazy? You can't have Sparky interview a murder suspect. He has all the diplomacy of..."

"Of what?"

"I can't come up with a good analogy. I can't imagine anyone, or *anything*, with as little tact as Sparky has."

"A crocodile?"

"Sure. Sparky is as diplomatic as a crocodile attacking a wildebeest."

"That's a little harsh."

Pinching the bridge of my nose, I said, "I can't believe we're having this conversation. Can we get back to something related to Astrid's murder?"

"Her alleged murder."

"When will you have the medical examiner's report on Astrid's death to prove it's a murder?"

"Astrid was cremated. There's nothing to examine unless we find someone who can read her ashes like they're tea leaves."

Ignoring the tea leaves comment, I asked, "You're really not planning to have the BCA collect fingerprints from my office?"

"No."

"I guess tomorrow's job will be picking up and sorting piles of paper."

As he parked in front of my house, Kerry said, "Talk to the dentist. It'll break up your day."

"My days are broken enough without doing your interviews."

"You know what I mean."

Getting out of Kerry's car, I held the door open for an extra moment. "You don't understand boundaries. I have a job, and it doesn't include interviewing murderers."

"He's only a suspect."

"Right. Innocent until proven guilty. Just the same, I'm not interested in questioning the dentist."

"Just think about it overnight. Get back to me tomorrow."

Kerry pulled forward, jerking the car door out of my hand before I could repeat my refusal. Inside, Jenny looked up from a sudoku puzzle when I walked in. "What happened at Whistling Pines?"

"Someone broke into my office and went through the drawers."

"Why?"

"I think they were looking for Astrid's puzzle box."

"Was it gone?"

"It's in the trunk of my car," I replied as I sat across the table from her.

"This puzzle box thing is getting crazy. When are you going to open it?"

"That's the problem! I can't get it open."

"Isn't there a YouTube video that'll show you how to open the box?"

"I think they're each unique."

Jenny stood and walked around the table. Kissing the top of my head, she said, "Come to bed. Things will look better in the light of day."

As I followed Jenny up the stairs, I glanced up at her cute bottom as it shifted under her pajamas. "The kids are asleep, right?"

Reading my mind, she said, "Forget it. We both have to work tomorrow."

"A little friendly necking would take my mind off the assignment Kerry gave me."

"What did Kerry assign you?" Jenny asked as she slid under the sheets.

"He wants me to interview the dentist who swapped out the oxygen cylinder."

"Why doesn't he do that himself?"

I slid into bed and turned off the nightstand light. "He thinks I might catch the dentist in an unguarded moment." I rolled against Jenny's back and spooned with her.

"I think having you interview a killer is a really bad idea." Grabbing my hand that was rubbing her stomach, Jenny bent my fingers back. "And trying to get frisky when I'm really tired would be a second bad idea."

Snuggling close I said, "I need something to take my mind off the potential dentist interview."

"There's a half-completed sudoku on the dining room table." She threw back the covers. "Come back to bed after I'm asleep."

Chapter 8

My morning routine was interrupted by a knock on the back door. I opened the door to Sparky's smiling face. "Thanks, Doc."

"Did our advice work?"

Sparky walked in. He helped himself to the cup of coffee I'd poured for myself and left sitting on the counter. "I apologized and suggested we go out for supper. Wendy smiled and was happy all evening."

I took down a second mug and poured myself a fresh cup. "Did you ever discover why you needed to apologize?"

After opening the refrigerator and rummaging around, Sparky poured a dollop of milk into his mug. "I apparently forgot to ask you to be my best man."

Snorting halfway through a swallow of coffee, I choked, then wiped my face and shirt with a paper towel. "You were going to ask me to be your best man?"

"I told Wendy you'd say yes, so it wasn't an issue."

"Wouldn't one of the firemen be a more logical choice?"

That was apparently a touchy question because Sparky stared into his coffee, fingering the mug nervously. "Wendy vetoed having any of the firemen in the wedding party."

"Why?"

"Some of the younger firemen have a reputation for getting wild and crazy at bachelor parties."

"But Wendy's okay with a sailor planning your bachelor party?"

Nodding, Sparky said, "She says you're possibly the most boring person she knows." Realizing that comment might not be taken as a compliment, Sparky backpedaled. "She meant boring in the nicest possible way. You know, like when you accidentally walked in on the art class and didn't stare at the naked model's boobs."

"That was being gentlemanly."

Sparky flipped his fingers. "Whatever. Wendy's sure that a bachelor party planned by you won't result in any naked women, drug use, or..."

"Or what?"

"I can't remember what the third thing was. It was something less bad than having a naked dancer or using drugs. She wants to make sure I'm still a virgin after the party."

Checking to make sure Jeremy wasn't listening from the dining room, I shushed Sparky. "Unless Wendy is pregnant by immaculate conception, your virginity is no longer intact."

Sparky's frown stopped me. "Not remembering that third thing that wasn't supposed to happen is bugging me."

"I'm sure it'll be fine. I'll talk to Vern at the VFW. I'll make sure there won't be any dancing girls or drugs."

Sparky's head jerked up so fast he nearly slopped his coffee. "The third thing is actually two things."

"That would make four things."

"No, because they're kind of interrelated." He paused, I waited for further explanation. "Actually, those two things could be part of the first two things. In that sense, there might only be one thing."

"The last two things could be related to a stripper and illegal drugs, so they'd all be one thing?"

Sparky's head bobbed emphatically. "One of the firemen's bachelor parties had a nude tattoo artist who used drugs to numb the pain."

A vision of a burly, naked, tattooed, biker sprang to mind. "Tell me the tattoo artist was female."

"It was a bachelor party. Of course, the naked tattoo artist was female. A naked guy tattooing firemen would be weird." The thought made Sparky chuckle. "She was kind of cute. Well, aside from her pierced..."

Trying to move on before a new disgusting image was burned into my brain, I asked, "What was the fourth thing that Wendy forbids?"

"Piercings."

"Wendy has piercings and tattoos. I'm surprised you're not allowed to get any."

"I can get a tattoo or belly button ring whenever I want. Well, except for during my bachelor party or when I'm drunk. She's afraid I'll get an inappropriate tattoo on some visible body part or that her name would be spelled wrong. She also said something about no earrings."

"Got it. No strippers, naked tattoo artists, drugs, earrings, or piercings."

"Wendy said it would be okay if we had a waxing party."

Jeremy, still half asleep, chose that moment to walk into the kitchen in search of his breakfast. "A wax party, like making candles?" he asked as he took down a bowl and filled it with cereal.

I stopped Sparky's answer. "That's a great suggestion. I'll tell Wendy we're going to make candles."

"I'm pretty sure Wendy meant hair removal waxing."

Jeremy stopped, trying to visualize hair removal with wax.

"Remember how Mom plucks her eyebrows? Well, people use wax to pull out the odd hairs."

Jeremy cocked his head and asked, "Doesn't that hurt?"

"I imagine it does."

Sparky nodded. "It hurts like hell." Seeing my glare, Sparky backed up. "It hurts like all heck."

Satisfied with that answer, Jeremy poured milk on his cereal and carried his bowl into the dining room.

Perplexed by the change of direction, Sparky said, "I think Wendy was talking about waxing body hair, not eyebrows."

I put a finger to my lips. "My son doesn't need to be exposed to the concept of a Brazilian wax job at his age."

"I think there will only be Swedes and Norwegians at the party. So, it'll mainly be Norwegian wax jobs."

I took Sparky's mug and placed it in the sink. "I'll be the best man, and you'll have the most boring bachelor party ever held in Two Harbors." I stopped Sparky at the door. "The wedding is Saturday, right? I should reserve the VFW back room for tomorrow night."

Sparky looked stunned. "It's already Thursday?"

"Yes, you're getting married in two days."

"I'd better tell the firemen."

Thinking about the firemen's reputation for wild partying, I asked, "Do you have any less rowdy friends I could invite to the bachelor party?"

Blinking, Sparky asked, "Besides you?"

"Yes, in addition to me. Are there a few other less rowdy guys you know?"

"I suppose I could invite Pastor Olafson and Stella Hygge."

"I'm not sure it's appropriate to invite a woman to a bachelor party. Folks might think she is part of the entertainment."

"Good point. I'll tell Stella not to come. I wouldn't want to tarnish her reputation."

Changing the topic, I asked, "What do you know about Dr. Robertson, the Beaver Bay dentist?"

"I don't hear much about him. I think the people in town go to either Dr. Eastman or Hilgren. As I recall, Dr. Robertson's patient base was the older folks. He liked to use laughing gas instead of Novocain because it was less expensive. And he never progressed past using silver fillings."

"Is he a nice guy or more of a jerk?"

"He always seemed nice enough, although it's hard to tell when you're high on laughing gas."

I walked Sparky as far as the driveway and said goodbye. Thinking about the security of the puzzle box, I decided to move it into the house and retrieve it from the car trunk. Jeremy watched me lock the box in the china hutch. "Do you think it'll be safe there?"

"I hope so," I replied. "I'll move it once I decide how best to open it."

"You can learn how to do anything on YouTube, Dad."

Feeling the need to accept Jeremy's sincere suggestion, while sure it was futile, I said, "I'll give YouTube a try tonight."

* * *

When I arrived, Bingle, the Whistling Pines maintenance man, was repairing my broken office door. "Thanks for taking care of me," I said as I stood by, dreading the impending task of picking up and sorting the hundreds of documents strewn around my office.

"No problem," Bingle replied in Swedish-accented English. "I can't replace the broken door frame today, but I'll put a couple of screws in the broken pieces, and it'll be somewhat secure."

"Secure enough to keep an honest person honest."

"Oh, that's a good one. Honest folks sometimes need a reminder to keep their hands off other peoples' things," Bingle replied as he used a cordless drill to drive a screw into a long piece of the door frame. "Say, why don't you get a cup of coffee? It'll take me a few more minutes to finish this repair and pack up my tools. Then I'll be out of your way."

I walked to the dining room and drew a cup of coffee from the urn before surveying the area. As usual, a few residents lingered after finishing their breakfasts, most socializing, others playing a game of cards or working on a jigsaw puzzle. Wendy was in the back corner, focused on a crossword puzzle. She looked up when I pulled out a chair to sit next to her. "I need a seven-letter word for 'darkened.'"

"Try obscure," I suggested.

While penciling the letters, Wendy shook her head. "How does that make any sense at all, and why do you know that?"

"I have a crossword kind of mind." As she finished writing, I asked, "Are you set for the wedding?"

"I may kill the groom before Saturday."

"If you're serious, I suggest not announcing that plan. It would indicate premeditation which would result in a longer jail term than a second-degree murder conviction, murder in the heat of an argument, or some other crime."

Tapping the eraser end of her #2 pencil on the crossword, Wendy glared at me. "I might need an accomplice to dispose of Sparky's body. What are you doing after supper?"

"What's wrong?"

Setting her pencil down, Wendy started ticking off items on her fingers. "Having Sparky underfoot all the time is annoying. Sparky's mother is domineering and possessive. I'm sick every morning. I have to pee all the time. Nothing tastes right, and I crave strange things. The seamstress has altered my wedding dress three times because my stomach and boobs are getting bigger. I'm generally irritable and increasingly irrational."

Deciding to change the topic, I asked, "How's your voice?"

"What?"

"I thought we'd grab Sherry Vogel and sing some show tunes before the afternoon movie. I was going to show *The Sound of Music*."

A smile flickered on Wendy's lips. "Darn it! I was happy being unhappy, and now you've ruined it."

Standing, I said, "I'll find Sherry. Meet me in the community room in fifteen minutes. We'll rehearse and decide who sings which duets."

"I think you have to sing "Maria" as a solo." Wendy stood, then asked, "When did you last play any of those songs?"

"It's been a couple of years. Why?"

"Do you feel comfortable performing them with only a few minutes of rehearsal?"

"It's not like we're performing at Carnegie Hall. Hell, half the residents are deaf."

Wendy smiled, breaking her somber mood. "And the other half are tone deaf."

I found Sherry chatting with two of the women getting their hair done in our little hair salon/barber shop. "We're going to perform songs from *The Sound of Music*."

Sherry excused herself and followed me into the hallway. "I know the songs, but not more than the first verse. And I don't know them well enough to perform them anywhere but in my shower."

"Sherry, you're a breath of fresh air for them. You're young, spunky, and funny. You provide a bit of sunlight in their dingy monotony."

"Is that my job description? Being a ray of sunshine?"

"If that's your job description, you're performing admirably."

Sherry was quiet while we walked to my office. "Actually, my dad asked how my job was going. I told him I was having fun. He asked if I was meeting your expectations."

"You're here on time every day. You make people happy. You fill in when I get dragged away. Those are all the things I expect of you."

"Dad seemed to think it was wrong that I was having fun. I guess he assumed a job should be...work."

"You're blessed with one of those rare jobs where you earn money, contribute, and have fun. Enjoy it while you can."

"Are you saying this will change, and I won't enjoy it anymore?"

I stopped where we were out of earshot of any residents and crossed my arms. "The hardest part of this job will be when one of your favorite people dies."

"I hadn't considered that."

"It's a fact that people here are nearing the end of their lives. Someone disappears to the hospital or dies every few months. It's our job to deal with that. Their friends and tablemates will be sad, and we need to help them cope. Even when we're sad ourselves."

"That sucks."

"It sometimes sucks. As staff members, we need to help the others cope with the loss, even when we're crying inside ourselves."

At my office, we stopped, and I admired Bingle's door repair. Sherry peeked past me and gasped. "It looks like a bomb went off in there."

"I'll have to deal with that mess later. Let's get my guitar and we'll meet Wendy in the community room."

Sherry seemed consumed with something on her phone.

"What are you up to?"

"I'm looking up song lyrics. They're all online."

We were into our third song when my cell phone vibrated. Excusing myself, I stepped aside. "This is Peter."

"Have you spoken with the dentist yet?" Kerry asked.

"I've been busy."

"Ah, did you get your office mess cleaned up?"

"Not yet. Say, can I call you back. They're ready for me to sing "Maria.""

"What are you talking about?"

"Wendy, Sherry, and I are singing songs before showing *The Sound of Music.*"

Sighing, Kerry said, "Call the dentist and make an appointment. Okay?"

"I need to plan Sparky's bachelor party."

"What bachelor party?"

"Sparky asked me to be his best man. I need to arrange a bachelor party for tomorrow night. You should plan on attending."

"I think having the police chief at the party might put a damper on the fun."

"It's going to be low-key. Wendy has forbidden strippers, tattoos, piercings, and anything else that might cause a permanent injury to Sparky or their relationship. Having you at the party might be the damper I need to keep things mild instead of wild."

"How would a stripper cause permanent injury?"

"I think the permanent injury would be Wendy's reaction to there being a stripper at the bachelor party." I paused. "Come to think of it, I'm unclear whether that threat was aimed at Sparky or at me as the party organizer."

"This is short notice. I don't know what venue you'll be able to find in a day."

"I'll call the VFW. I bet Vern will let us use the back room or a quiet corner."

"Find a sober driver or two. I don't want Sparky to spend the night in the county jail after I arrest him for driving while intoxicated. I trust you to have the good sense not to drink and drive."

I ended the call and punched in the VFW's phone number. "Vern, I'm planning Sparky's bachelor party for tomorrow night. Can we use the back room?"

Vern, the VFW manager, chuckled. "Tomorrow is the meat raffle. I don't think that's compatible with a bachelor party and stripper. Although, a lot of my patrons might enjoy seeing a partially naked woman dancing around the place. It'd certainly liven up the crowd."

"There's not going to be a stripper. It will be the most boring bachelor party in the history of bachelor parties."

"Well, hell, I suppose having more people buying meat raffle tickets might lend some excitement to the evening."

I was suddenly aware of my lack of understanding. "I'm sorry, did you say you were hosting a meat raffle?"

"Yeah. We have one every Friday night."

"What *is* a meat raffle?"

"The ladies' auxiliary brings packages of meat, then sells raffle tickets. At eight o'clock, they draw names out of a basket and the winner gets his or her choice of the meat on display. The person with the ticket number one below the winner gets a free drink."

Suddenly recalling the donations of freezer-burned game for the preparation of booya, I froze. "What kind of meat are we talking about?"

"You know, the kind you'd get at Dahlberg's Butcher Shop. It's beef steaks, pork chops, chicken wings, and such. The two-pounds of thick-sliced bacon and homemade brats are usually favorites."

"And people buy tickets to get in on the drawing?"

"Sure. Wes Dahlberg sells the meat to us at cost, so everyone knows the event is a fundraiser."

"How much are the tickets?"

"They're $5 each or five tickets for $20."

"How many packages of meat are given away?"

"I'm not entirely sure. It seems like there are usually ten or a dozen. On most nights, about half the people go home with meat." Vern chuckled to himself. "There's usually a booby prize. The last ticket drawn gets a package of calf's liver or chicken giblets."

"I thought you were going to say a package of lutefisk."

"There's only lutefisk and pickled herring in December. It's the wrong season. Besides, those aren't booby prizes. The lutefisk is often the second or third package chosen."

"Back to tomorrow night. Bringing a bunch of firemen there for a bachelor party won't be a problem for your meat raffle?"

"Naw. You get those firemen liquored up, and they might be very generous with their raffle ticket purchases."

"What does the ladies' auxiliary do with the profits?"

"I think they buy material and batting, then sew quilts they donate to the Minnesota Veterans Hospital."

"Wow, that's very kind."

"Say, why don't you bring your guitar? You can sing songs between the drawings."

"I hadn't thought about it. I'm supposed to be keeping Sparky out of trouble."

"How much trouble can Sparky get into here at the VFW with a bunch of gray-haired veterans and their wives?"

"Is that a rhetorical question, or do you really want me to answer?"

Vern laughed. "The biggest excitement we'll have tomorrow night is the person who draws first and chooses the T-bone steaks. It's all downhill from there."

"But there will be firemen."

"Is Stella Hygge attending?"

"I don't know. Would that be a good or a bad thing?"

"Stella keeps those guys in line. She's just a little thing, but I overheard the guys talking about her, and they're convinced if one of them was injured and trapped inside a burning building, Stella would be the first one to rush in and carry them out."

"That's saying a lot."

"She's earned their respect. Better than that, she's earned the respect of the firemen's wives. She doesn't take shit from anyone. If you want this to be a boring, controlled party, make sure you invite Stella."

"Good suggestion. I'll give her a call."

The fire station non-emergency number rang three times before it was answered. "Fire hall."

"Stella?"

"Yeah, who's this?"

"I'm Peter Rogers. I was hoping you'd join us for Sparky's bachelor party tomorrow night."

"Is this a joke? Are you going to suggest that I pop out of a cake or something?"

"No! I have orders from Wendy to plan the most boring bachelor party that's ever been held."

"So, you're inviting me to be the fun sponge?"

"Fun sponge?" I asked.

"You know, the person who sucks the fun out of the celebration."

"Um, no. I'm inviting you because you're one of the firemen, and I thought you'd like to be part of the party."

Frowning, Stella asked, "Are you seriously inviting me to a bachelor party?"

"It's at the VFW tomorrow night." I paused, then added. "I think the firemen's wives would be relieved if you attended. You have a reputation for being a trustworthy and rational influence on the otherwise wild group."

Stella chuckled. "Yeah, that's me. Old trustworthy and rational. Are you serious about this being a boring and laid-back bachelor party?"

"It's going to be at the VFW during the meat raffle."

"There's not going to be a stripper or anything nasty?"

"I promise, there won't be a stripper. Like I said, the meat raffle will be the highlight of the evening."

"I've heard that you sometimes play guitar at Hugo's. Are you providing the entertainment tomorrow night?"

"The VFW manager asked me to bring my guitar."

"Do you know any country songs?"

"I know the great American songbook. You make your request, and I'll probably be able to fake my way through it."

"Cool! I'll be there."

As an afterthought, I asked, "Would you consider being a sober driver to make sure the guys get home safely?"

There was a pause, then Stella said, "Sure, but if any of them get handsy, there will be broken fingers."

"Fair enough!"

Chapter 9

Unlike Sparky, who politely knocked on our door and waited for me to let him in, Wendy knocked once and blew in like a Minnesota tornado. Luckily, or unluckily, depending on how you looked at it, the kids were still up. Jeremy barely glanced up from the television when she stormed into the living room before I'd had a chance to stand.

"You will not believe what that stupid fireman did this time!" she said as she took a chair without invitation.

I nodded toward Jeremy, hoping to head off one of Wendy's inappropriate for children's ears tirades. "What happened?"

"We were watching *Jeopardy!* and Ken Jennings has just given the final answer. With the tension building, Sparky turned to me and says, 'Nome, Alaska?'"

"Was that the solution?" I asked.

"Hell...er...heck no," she replied after glancing at Jeremy and softening her epithet. "That's not the point! He broke my concentration while I was trying to recall the answer."

"What was the final *Jeopardy!* question?" Jenny asked.

"Aren't you listening?" Wendy snapped. "The question is irrelevant. The interruption when another person is concentrating is…"

"Inappropriate?" I suggested.

"Impolite?" Jenny asked,

"Rude!" Wendy replied.

"What was the question?" Jenny asked again.

"It was the kickoff point for the gold rush."

"Ah," I said. "What is Skagway?"

"Of course, it was Skagway. I knew that, but Sparky's saying 'Nome' threw me off, and I couldn't recall Skagway before everyone had to put down their pen."

"Did all of the contestants get the correct answer?" Jenny asked.

"Neil Patrick Harris got it right, but Jimmy Kimmel and Melissa Rauch both guessed Nome."

Jenny stood and picked up Amy. "Wendy, I have a very important bit of marital advice. Pick your battles."

"What does that mean?"

As Jenny climbed the stairs, leaving the dumpster fire for me to put out, I replied, "Not everything is worth fighting about. The best pathway to marital bliss is to let little irritations pass and save your confrontations for the bigger issues that are basic to your personal beliefs."

"I disagree! Sparky needs to understand my very basic boundaries. If he can't respect my need to have silence while considering the final *Jeopardy!* question, how is he ever going to deal with my band practice schedule and my quiet time while doing crosswords?"

"Having a baby will change your priorities. You need to understand that a helpless child's needs will take precedence over *Jeopardy!*, crossword puzzles, and even band practice."

"What the...heck are you talking about? Those are some of the most basic of my needs."

"Your basic needs are food, water, a job, and sleep. And trust me, a kid will test your absolute minimum requirements for even those necessities. Everything in your life will become things that are nice but not required."

Wendy glanced at the stairs as if willing Jenny to return. "What in heck are you talking about, Peter? My basic needs won't change because I'm having a kid."

"Your whole life is about to change. Marriage does that and having a child compounds the changes. A screaming baby needs to be fed or changed regardless of your interest in a game show or crossword answer. Your meal might have to wait until your child is fed."

"This kid is Sparky's responsibility."

"I've got news for you. Sparky is a fireman, and when there's a call-out, he will leave."

Wendy struggled up from the chair and glared at me. "Thanks for nothing. If you're not going to be helpful, I'll seek answers elsewhere."

"Thank you," I said as she shuffled across the kitchen.

"What did you say?"

"I said, thank you. Take your problems elsewhere and see if you can get different answers from someone else."

"Fine! I will!"

"Why don't you have Sparky's mother move in to help you with the baby," I said.

"I won't give her the satisfaction of me asking for her help," Wendy said before slamming the door.

Jenny crept downstairs and peeked into the living room.

"She's gone. The coast is clear."

Jenny tapped Jeremy's shoulder. "Time for you to put on pajamas and brush your teeth."

In a welcome change, which had come about in the past few weeks, Jeremy nodded and went upstairs without argument or negotiation. Jenny sat down next to me. "Wendy needs an attitude adjustment before the baby arrives."

I glanced at the back door, just to make sure Wendy hadn't snuck back in. "She's got a real problem. She's lived alone, done what she's wanted to do, spent her money only on herself."

"Nodding, Jenny agreed. "She's led an isolated life."

"Isolated aside from the band groupies she shacked up with."

Jenny nudged me with her elbow. "You don't know that."

"I do know that. I've seen her flirting with guys in the audience and necking with them in the parking lots."

"That's all part of her schtick. Her persona."

"I'm pretty sure it wasn't an act," I replied.

"She's never hit on you."

Ignoring Wendy's one serious attempt at flirtation, I replied, "I have an effective force field that deflects all women who approach with amorous intentions."

Snorting, Jenny stood. "Like the cute redhead who stuck her tongue down your throat at Hugo's."

"Bobbie was an old friend."

"An old friend who wanted to jump your bones."

I turned off the living room lights and followed Jenny upstairs. "You stepped in and handled that situation."

"That's right. Your force field must've broken down that night."

"I did nothing to encourage her."

"You didn't appear to be pushing her away."

"She caught me off guard. I would've pushed her away and sent her packing if you hadn't stepped in."

"Yeah, right." Jenny flipped on the bedroom lights, then turned and put her arms around my neck. "Listen, just because you were a sailor doesn't mean you get to have a girl in every port or bar."

"I know that. I'm a one-woman sailor."

Jenny kissed me, then grabbed her pajamas off the bed. "Keep that in mind at tomorrow's bachelor party."

"That's not going to be a problem. We're having it at the VFW. All the women who'll be there are the wives of Vietnam vets."

"How about the stripper?" Jenny asked from the bathroom.

"There isn't going to be a stripper. Wendy has set down very strict rules. No stripper. No tattoos, earrings, or piercings. Nothing that will leave permanent marks on Sparky's body."

"And the firemen are going along with those plans?"

"Stella Hygge is going to help me enforce the rules and will be the sober driver."

"She's that cute female firefighter, right?"

"Yes."

"I've heard that she rides herd on those crazy firemen like a den mother."

"I guess they really like and respect her. She told me if any of the guys she drives home get fresh with her, she'll break their fingers."

Jenny appeared at the bed wearing cotton pajamas. "I like that in a woman who is driving home other women's husbands."

As I climbed under the covers, I kissed Jenny and said, "There's a meat raffle at the VFW, and Vern asked me to bring my guitar so I can sing a few songs between drawings."

Jenny pushed herself up. "There's a meat raffle during the bachelor party? A meat raffle meaning dates are being raffled off?"

"Nope. They're raffling off cuts of beef and pork. I guess the bacon and bratwurst packs are very popular."

Groaning, Jenny said, "I'll have nightmares about people bringing home slabs of meat that sat unrefrigerated on the VFW counter for the entire evening,"

"I'm sure they write names on the packages and keep them in the refrigerator."

"Do us a favor; don't buy any raffle tickets."

Chapter 10

The next morning, I brought the puzzle box to the Whistling Pine dining room. I drew a cup of coffee from the urn and surveyed the people who'd stayed behind to socialize and play cards after finishing breakfast. Kathy Christensen smiled and waved, so I took the empty seat at the table where she was seated with Karla Telker and Mary Gilbert. Kathy reached out and took the puzzle box from me. "How close have you come to opening the box?"

"The locksmith had it open. Hulda thought it looked messy, so she closed the box before anyone saw what was inside."

Karla watched Kathy manipulate the small slides on the two ends of the box. "That sounds like something Hulda would do. I'm sure my mother would've had the same reaction. She liked things to be neat."

Nodding, Mary agreed. "My mother-in-law always joined us for Sunday dinner and holidays. Everything was expected to be in its proper place. I'd race around the living room, straightening the magazines. After that, I'd make sure there was enough toilet paper on the rolls."

"Your mother-in-law cared how much toilet paper was on the rolls?" I asked as I watched Kathy slide the puzzle box lid a quarter of an inch to the side, where it stopped.

"One Sunday, we were in the middle of a chicken dinner when 'nature called.' My mother-in-law toddled to the toilet as we ate. I was about to put a forkful of mashed potatoes in my mouth when she called out, 'You're out of toilet paper in here. Should I use the magazine?' After that, I made sure there was always a full roll of toilet paper hung in the guest bathroom before family dinners."

Unable to move any more of the slides, Kathy handed the box back to me. "I'm stuck there."

"That seems to be the endpoint most people hit," I replied. "I can see the edge of a folded sheet of paper, but I can't read or remove it."

Karla took the puzzle box from Kathy and considered the small opening. Shaking the box, we could hear the paper moving around inside. Looking up, Karla surveyed the room, then called out to Megan Powers. "Meg, do you have a crochet hook in your purse?"

Megan rose from her chair and walked over from a nearby table. Setting her suitcase-sized purse on the table, she dug through the contents. "I'm sure there's a crochet hook somewhere in here." She produced a long rod with a notch cut into the end. "Here you go."

Accepting the crochet hook, Karla shook the box to shift the folded paper to the opening. Using the notch on the crochet hook, she manipulated it inside the box until she caught the paper's folded edge. Carefully twisting the box, she gently tugged until the tiniest corner of the yellowed paper emerged. "Can you grab that, Peter?"

Using my fingernails, I tried unsuccessfully to grasp the tiny, exposed sliver of paper. Intrigued by the activity, residents from nearby tables gathered around us. "I've got tweezers!" Jeri Westfall said. She dashed away from the crowd, returning with silver tweezers she handed to Mary. "Here, you have the steadiest hands."

Using the tweezers, Mary pinched the exposed corner. "Okay, Karla, pull the crochet hook out." With the crochet hook out of the way, Mary slid the paper back and forth, a bit more exposed with each motion. "I want to get a better grasp on the paper to pull without tearing it but I'm afraid to let go."

Megan handed Karla a safety pin, and she carefully used the point to anchor the paper against the wooden box. Mary adjusted her grasp, pinched a larger corner of the paper and slid it back and forth. Unable to coax it any farther, she drew a breath. "I might be able to pull it free," she said, as she paused.

"But I might tear off the corner. What would you like me to do, Peter?"

"Go ahead and pull," I replied. "We've got nothing to lose at this point."

Mary gently slid the exposed paper to the side of the box, so the edge was aligned with the opening and pulled. To my surprise, the yellowed paper had enough strength to slide through the opening.

With a tiny edge showing, Karla pinned the exposed edge with her fingernail. "Get a better grasp, Mary."

Everyone was on the edge of their chairs as Mary released the tweezers to get a better purchase on the exposed edge. After taking a deep breath, Mary wiggled the paper side-to-side as she pulled the paper from the box. With a quarter inch now showing, she set aside the tweezers and gripped the edge with her fingers. It took nearly another minute, but she was able to pull the entire folded sheet out of the box.

I laughed when the gathered crowd started clapping. Accepting the folded sheet from Mary, I carefully unfolded it."

"What does it say?" Kathy asked.

Momentarily stunned by the revelation of the contents, I paused. "These are the directions for opening the box."

Mary led the laughter. "Who would put the solution to opening a puzzle box inside of the box?"

"I suppose Astrid didn't want to lose them," Kathy replied.

Lifting the box from the table, I made the series of slides indicated by the directions, and within a minute, I had the box fully open. "Tada!" I said.

Mary gestured for me to hand her the box. After turning the box side to side and end to end, she cocked her head. "The bottom is too thick. Do the directions show you how to open another layer?"

"The directions show pushing in the lowest layer of end slides, which should allow the bottom to slide over. There's no indication of another compartment."

As suggested, Kathy pushed the lower slides inward a quarter inch. After that, she slid the bottom panel, and another sheet of paper fell out. Everyone stared at the newly exposed sheet of paper, as if afraid to touch it.

"Maybe it's cursed, like the mummy's tomb," Hulda said from the back of the crowd.

Karla grimaced, as if she had a sudden migraine. She picked up the paper and unfolded it. She snorted, then handed it to me. "It's a treasure map. Right down to *X marks the spot.*"

As Karla said, the sheet of paper was a map, showing the direction and number of paces to make from a series of landmarks. Unfortunately, there was no indication of where in the world the map was set.

"Where's the treasure?" Hulda asked.

Howard Johnson, intrigued by the gathering crowd, joined us in the dining room. Being among the most experienced local experts, and relatively sane, I handed the map to him. "Do you know where this map is set?"

Accepting the paper, Howard quickly scanned it. "Eugene might've hidden something in Korea, intending to return some day to retrieve it."

"Bah," Hulda replied. "He was crooked. I bet he shipped something home from Korea and stashed it somewhere locally."

Handing the map back to me, Howard shrugged. "A lot of things stolen from Korea were too valuable to display for sale. Perhaps Eugene planned to sell some items to a private investor."

"Why hide it?" I asked.

"People become focused on more recent news. Maybe Eugene was waiting for interest in stolen Korean goods to wane."

I stared at the map. "How large of an item do you think he hid?"

"Something small enough to carry home in an Army footlocker," Howard replied. "So, smaller than a bread box."

"Did soldiers really steal artifacts and things, then take them home?" Kathy asked.

Howard nodded. "Sadly, yes. In every war there are tens of thousands of treasures and artifacts looted by soldiers. I'd like to think our servicemen were more ethical than most. In reality, there were thousands of soldiers in Korea exposed to unimaginable mayhem and destruction. With houses, cities, museums, and churches being destroyed, I know many treasures were pocketed by soldiers and civilians walking through."

Nodding, I said, "The U.S. just returned Queen Munjeong's royal seal, from the Josean Dynasty. It had apparently been taken by an American soldier during the Korean Conflict."

Karla leaned back. "So, Eugene might've stashed something that was worth millions of dollars?"

"According to the internet, there are still more than 100,000 artifacts missing from Korea. Experts assume most of them are either in the U.S. or North Korea, although some have turned up in Australia, Canada, and England."

Kathy's eyes sparkled. "We can have an honest-to-god treasure hunt! Peter, make copies of the map!"

"I think the police chief needs to deal with this," I replied, refolding the map and placing it into my pocket.

The crowd was breaking up when my cell phone vibrated. The screen displayed a reminder message, *Dentist appointment in 30 minutes.*

"What dentist appointment?" I said to myself. I entered the phone number from the text and waited while it rang twice.

A female voice answered, "Dental office."

"I just received a reminder that I have an appointment in thirty minutes. I don't recall making a dental appointment."

"Who is this?" the woman asked.

"My name is Peter Rogers."

"Yes, Mr. Rogers. You have a 9:30 appointment."

"I don't recall making an appointment."

"Your wife made the appointment for you. She called this morning, and we were able to squeeze you into the schedule."

Confused, I asked the first question that came to mind. "Which dental office am I scheduled at?"

"You have an appointment with Dr. Robertson in Beaver Bay."

I sighed, suddenly aware of Kerry's conspiracy to have me interview Astrid's nephew. "Thank you. I'll leave right now."

Dialing Jenny's cell phone as I walked to the car, I steamed. "How much did Kerry pay you to make a dental appointment for me?"

"He didn't pay me anything. He explained that you were going to interview Dr. Robertson and he asked if I'd call to make an appointment for you."

"Why didn't you tell me?"

"I sent you a calendar entry when you didn't answer your phone. Is your phone off, or did you just turn off the ringer?"

I lowered the phone and touched the ring tone icon, which displayed a diagonal line through a bell. "I inadvertently turned off the ringer," I replied. "You could've walked down and warned me."

"Listen, *dear,* I have a full-time job that requires my attention to detail. I'm not able to wander around the place, having coffee with the residents, like some members of the staff."

"Fine. I'm on my way to Beaver Bay."

"Perfect. Ask the dentist about your one remaining wisdom tooth. Maybe he'll extract it for you."

"I'm not having a semi-retired dentist who confuses oxygen with nitrous oxide pull one of my teeth."

Ending the call as I got into the car, I steamed as I drove toward Beaver Bay. *I need to have a discussion with Kerry about boundaries.*

* * *

I found the dental office in a strip mall, which was pretty much all there was to downtown Beaver Bay. The entrance was nestled between a souvenir shop specializing in polished Lake Superior agates and Thomsonite, and a convenience store selling everything from snack foods to beer.

A white-haired woman in blue scrubs looked up from her computer when I walked in. Her expression seemed to show unusual surprise, considering I was on time for my appointment. As I approached the desk, I realized she'd had a facelift, and her look of

141

surprise was a byproduct of the plastic surgeon over-tightening her forehead. The surgery also lifted her eyebrows about half an inch too high. She'd plucked them, then penciled in an eyebrow line in a more natural location.

"Peter Rogers, I assume. Do you have your dental insurance information handy?"

After digging through the assorted cards in my wallet, I handed her the card for my Whistling Pines dental policy. The receptionist entered my policy information into her computer ever so slowly, looking at the card after every keystroke, as if she couldn't remember the entire words *Delta* and *Dental*. It seemed to take her five minutes to enter the policy number. "You could finish that while I'm with the dentist," I suggested.

"No. The dentist doesn't see anyone until I've verified their insurance, or they've prepaid for their examination."

"So, you'll have to call the insurance company before I'll be seen?"

The woman snorted. "Of course not. Once I get your number into our system, I'll log onto their website and enter your ID."

Closing my eyes while trying to maintain my composure, I said, "I'll take a seat."

"Good idea."

Ten minutes later, I'd finished reading an article about steelhead trout fishing and had moved on to an article about the history of commercial herring fishing.

"Mr. Rogers."

I stood and approached the receptionist's desk, expecting to be shown to an exam room. "Yes?"

"Is this your most current card? It seems that the insurance company doesn't have your coverage."

"It's the only dental insurance card I've ever had. It never changes."

"Hang on," she said, removing a magnifying glass from the desk's lap drawer.

Grimacing, I watched as she used her fingertip to follow the numbers she'd entered on the computer while she read the magnified numbers from my card.

"Can you tell if this is an eight or a six?" she asked, pointing to the fifth digit in my identification number.

"Actually, I think it's a zero. You know, an 'O' with a slash across it so you'd know it's a zero."

She moved the magnifying glass in and out, trying to improve the focus. "I think it's an eight and I'd entered it as a six. Let me try that new number."

I watched her backspace to the incorrect number, which she changed. Then she started re-entering the rest of the numbers, one digit at a time.

"I could read the numbers to you," I suggested.

"That would be unethical," she replied as she continued to read the numbers with the magnifying glass, then adding them to the ID number one digit at a time.

The outside door opened, and Brian Johnson swept in, interrupting the woman's concentration. "Hi, Doc," he said to me as he walked up to the receptionist.

"Mr. Johnson," the woman said, turning to look at her desktop calendar. "You're a little early. Since I'm having difficulty finding this patient's insurance information for his 9:30 appointment, why don't you go right in?"

Brian smiled at me. "I didn't expect to see you here, Doc. Most of Dr. Robertson's patients are people who've been seeing him since they were children."

The receptionist looked up at me, raising her eyebrows to an even higher level on her forehead. "You're a doctor?"

Brian jumped in before I could reply. "Peter is also a decorated veteran who served with the Marines in Iraq."

The receptionist stood and extended her hand. "Thanks for your service. Dr. Robertson extends medical courtesy to fellow professionals." She handed me the insurance card she'd been working on for nearly fifteen minutes. "Let me get Dr. Robertson."

With the receptionist gone, I whispered, "I'm not a doctor."

Brian whispered back, "And Dr. Robertson shouldn't be practicing dentistry. I guess the two of you are even."

"If he's incompetent, why are you here?"

"I'm here for a cleaning with Carmen. The dentist who does my fillings and crowns gets backed up. Dr. Robertson and his dental hygienist always have openings."

The receptionist reappeared, apparently smiling, although, with her taut face and apparent Botox injections, it was hard to tell just which expression she was showing. "Both of you can go in now."

Through the door behind the receptionist was a cramped space with side-by-side dental chairs. A woman, who appeared to be somewhat younger than the receptionist, was setting up a tray for Brian's teeth cleaning. She smiled and gestured for him to take the nearest chair.

Seated next to the other chair was an elderly white-haired man I recognized from the church's video of Astrid's event. He smiled and gestured toward the second chair. "You must be Dr. Rogers. I don't think we've met."

I was about to correct the perception that I was a medical professional when Brian interrupted. "Doc is a real hero. He served with the Marines in Iraq and still has some shrapnel in his shoulder."

Robertson straightened and smiled. "I'm always pleased to have a patient who served in our armed forces. It's an honor to meet you, Dr. Rogers."

"Please call me Peter," I said as I sat in the exam chair.

"What can I do for you today? Your wife told my receptionist you were having problems with a wisdom tooth."

"It's not so much a problem, as it's the only wisdom tooth I have left. I was wondering if it's sound, or if I should have it extracted."

My chair leaned back, and the doctor spread a paper napkin on my chest. "Open wide. We'll take a look at that bad boy."

"Do you often use nitrous oxide?" I asked before opening my mouth wide.

"I find that nitrous oxide takes the edge off for people who are anxious about their procedures. It's one of the tools in my toolbox."

In between oral invasions, Brian spoke up. "Peter works with the Whistling Pines residents. Isn't that where your Aunt Astrid's piano was donated?"

It felt like a tiny hammer was striking my back tooth. Sitting up, the dentist said, "I think we should take an x-ray of your tooth. It seems sound, but I'd like to be certain."

As the doctor set up for my x-ray, he said, "Yes, I believe Aunt Astrid's piano was donated to the senior residence in Two Harbors."

"Peter, wasn't there some kind of box found inside the piano?"

After glaring at Brian, I said, "Yes, the piano tuner found an oriental puzzle box in the piano."

Robertson stopped his x-ray preparation. "What do you know about that box?"

"No one seems to be able to open it."

Robertson relaxed and resumed his preparation. "That box is actually part of my aunt's estate. Its inclusion in the donated piano was an oversight. I'd appreciate any influence you could use to have it returned to me, the executor of the estate."

"I was told the box was part of the piano donation. I think Whistling Pines is planning to donate it to the county historical society."

"Perhaps the old folks' home would accept a generous donation for returning the box back to the estate. I'm sure there are many places where a few hundred dollars could be put to good use. Where are you storing the box? I think it needs to be in a humidity-controlled room to preserve the wood."

"It seems odd that Astrid would store something so delicate and valuable inside an old piano," I replied.

"It's not very valuable," the dentist said, now ignoring my x-ray. "There's sentimental value. My Uncle Eugene brought that box back from Korea. We'd like to keep it in the family." Robertson paused. "Where are you storing it?"

"Is it still in your office, Doc?" Brian asked.

That question totally captivated the dentist. "In *your* office?"

"We've turned it over to the police for safekeeping."

"You've involved the police in the storage of an antique box?"

"Someone broke into my office, apparently searching for the box or something. We decided it would be prudent to keep it somewhere secure." I sat up.

"You said no one has been able to open it yet?" he asked, sounding hopeful.

"Do you think there's something valuable inside, Dr. Robertson?"

"I wouldn't know," the dentist replied. "Uncle Eugene was rather circumspect when he discussed the box and certain other things he'd liberated from Korea at the end of the war."

"Liberated?" I asked.

"Uncle Eugene was part of the force that pushed all the way to the Chinese border. He understood that North Korea would probably come under Chinese control at some point. With them being heathens, he decided it would be best to save some of their religious relics from destruction."

"What, specifically, did he liberate?" I asked.

"He never specified which items he had. Nor did he tell the family where they were stored."

"And you think the answers may be inside the puzzle box?"

"That's one theory."

"Your aunt's death was very suspicious,"
I said.

"Not at all. She was slowly dying of
COPD. She collapsed during a church service
and died."

"It appears her oxygen bottle ran out and
a new bottle was swapped just prior to her
death."

"Are you an undercover police officer,
sir?" Robertson asked.

Choking on something, Brian sat up and
spit into the porcelain basin. "No. I can
vouch for Doc. He's about as far from being
a cop as you and I are."

"Then, why are you asking about my
aunt's unfortunate death?"

"I watched the church service on their
website. It appears that someone, who
looked a lot like you, swapped her empty
oxygen cylinder for a nitrous oxide cylinder
shortly before her collapse."

"Nitrous oxide isn't poisonous. Why
would a mistake like that cause concern?"

"If she was having breathing problems,
and her supplemental oxygen was changed
out for nitrous oxide, she might've
suffocated."

Brian was sitting on the edge of the chair
while Carmen watched, equally intrigued by
the discussion. "Yeah, she might've
suffocated. I've heard that states are even
considering the use of pure nitrogen to
execute prisoners. They keep breathing as if
nothing is wrong, right up until their brains

shut down because they're not getting oxygen."

Robertson's face turned red, and he stood. "Both of you can leave."

"Guilty conscience?" Brian asked.

"I feel like I'm being accused of something when nothing untoward happened. I've lost my aunt, and I don't need to relive that loss, much less to be accused of something."

I stood and said, "Someone thought the puzzle box was in my office, broke in, and searched my desk."

"I don't know anything about that," Robertson replied. "Leave now."

As we walked out, Brian looked over his shoulder. "Do you think he'll bill my insurance for the cleaning?"

"Brian!"

"What? Carmen never finished my cleaning. And I didn't get a new toothbrush."

"I'm more concerned about Robertson's involvement in his aunt's death and his interest in the puzzle box."

Chapter 11

I was still riled up over the Robertson confrontation when I got back to Whistling Pines. Sherry met me at the front door. "We're ready to start the movie, and you said we were going to sing first."

As we hurried down the hallway, I asked, "Have you made popcorn?"

"The popcorn is made, and people are seated and restless. Everything is ready, but we couldn't find you."

We swept into the community room, which was buzzing with conversation. Wendy quieted the group as I took my guitar out of the case. "Who would like to hear some of the songs from *The Sound of Music*?"

Quiet applause followed and Wendy leaned over. "Sing "Maria.""

I played the opening chords, then sang a solo. Following that, Wendy and Sherry joined me in "Edelweiss" and "Sixteen Going on Seventeen." The seniors clapped and those who knew the words sang along. After five songs, we ended the concert. Sherry started the movie as I dimmed the lights.

With the movie showing, Sherry, Wendy, and I slipped out the back and closed the door. Wendy wandered away as I put my guitar into its case. Sherry watched silently until I snapped the latches. "I really like this part of my job. I mean, who gets paid to sing at work?"

Picking up the guitar case, I nodded toward the hallway. "Follow me back to my office."

"Is there something more I should be doing?"

"I think you're doing very well. I'd like to involve you in more of the recreation planning."

"Like what?"

"I create a monthly events schedule. That includes repetitive things, like the weekly movies, but also requires me to seek out other enrichment opportunities."

"Like the art class," she said.

"Yes, that's one example. I need to find things that add variety. Things to stimulate interest and engage people."

"The Halloween events did that."

Stepping into my office, I set the guitar case in the corner. "That's a great example of using outside events to enrich our internal activities. Think of some more things for this summer."

Sherry sat in my chair and leaned forward as she counted off ideas. "There really isn't much between July 4th and Labor Day."

"Be creative. What else is going on in town and in the region?"

"We could take a group out fishing."

"That's a possibility, although it's usually cold on Lake Superior, and there's the cost of a charter boat and fishing licenses. That's a good example of something regional. What else is there?"

"Tourists flock to Gooseberry Falls and Split Rock Lighthouse. We could take a group of people on a field trip to see them."

"Perfect!" I said, handing her a pencil and a blank calendar. "You put together a plan for next month. Start with our usual weekly and monthly activities, then add a couple of extra items. A field trip would be great. Figure out how long it would take to drive there and give the residents time to check out the site, then to drive back. That'll determine when you have to start."

Sherry looked surprised. "You fit everything in between meals, don't you?"

"I try to. Although, the residents do enjoy taking a field trip that includes buying lunch somewhere or stopping for coffee or pie. If you put those into the plan, you'll have to contact the restaurant to choose a time that's not too busy, so a vanload of slow-moving senior citizens won't mess up their usual customers."

"Wow, this is harder than I'd guessed. You make it seem so easy."

Smiling, I nodded. "That's the secret to this job. You put in all the work up front, so the events are easy for the participants."

"I suppose it's extra hard because some of the residents don't move fast."

"Nor do they respond to structured plans. There's always someone who's late, lost, or in the bathroom when you're ready to move on."

Sherry giggled. "I overheard you tell the director our job was herding squirrels."

"It sometimes seems like that. But through it all, we have to appear upbeat and in control of the situation. No matter how things have turned to manure, you have to pretend that you're above it and keep everything moving."

Sherry stood, then stopped at the door. "That's what you did when you saw me modeling for the art class, isn't it?"

"I pretended I wasn't shocked, and I tried to keep things moving ahead as we'd planned."

"I talked to my mom about that day. She said you handled things like a real professional."

"That's about the nicest compliment I've ever received. Thank her for me."

Sherry nodded, then added, "And, you're a gentleman."

"Thank you."

After Sherry left, I unlocked my desk and removed the puzzle box from the drawer and removed the map. Feeling uneasy that I was holding the only copy, and knowing that someone, possibly Dr. Robertson, had already searched my office for the box, I scanned the map and saved a copy onto my computer. I attached the map to an email and sent copies to Kerry, Nancy, Jenny, and myself, reasoning that having a copy on the internet assured access to the document even if the original was stolen or lost.

The printer was whirring as Brian Johnson stepped into my office and sat in my guest chair. "What instrument do sheep play?"

Unprepared for Brian's arrival or the question, I shrugged.

"Tubaas," he said, drawing out the baaing sheep sound. Brian laughed as I groaned. "Write that one down for your son."

"I think I'll remember that one. Is there something I can do for you?"

"You said you'd found a map in the puzzle box but didn't know what location it described."

After a moment of hesitation, I handed Brian the copy I'd printed. "Please consider this information confidential."

"You having the map is hardly a secret," he said as he looked at the paper. "And not knowing the starting point, makes it useless."

"It seems straight forward," I said, holding the original. "It appears the starting point is..." I studied the indecipherable scribbles. "I can make out what looks like 'Norwegian.'"

Brian twisted the map to read it from a slightly different angle. "It appears there's some sort of structure that's either square or rectangular. I think it says, 'Crazy Norwegian's place.'"

"All we have to do is find a crazy Norwegian's house, then go thirty yards northwest to some shrub, tree, or cloud."

Brian's eyebrows went up. "Describing the property owner as a crazy Norwegian would include roughly half of the people in Two Harbors, the other half being crazy Swedes."

"The person who drew this up must've had someone specific in mind. Was there some 1950s Norwegian who was crazier than the rest or went by the nickname 'Crazy?'"

"I'm probably the wrong person to ask. Back then, people used nicknames like Crazy, among themselves, not around kids like me. Although, my dad *did* use nicknames when he spoke about his drinking buddies. There were Buzz, Speed, Blinkers, and Judd. I don't remember anyone nicknamed Crazy, although he did refer to several people as crazy, stupid, or lame brained."

I snatched the map from Brian's hand. "Thanks for your help."

"You need to practice your sarcasm. That came off as a little too sharp. Good sarcasm is as smooth as diplomacy. You want to smile when you hand someone a scoop of manure, like they're receiving a gift."

"I'll keep that in mind."

"We've got band practice tonight. Are you planning to attend?"

"I'm really too busy to play in the band."

"We have openings for sax and piccolo players. You could fill in on either instrument."

"I haven't played the piccolo since the Sousa concert."

Brian stepped toward the door, then paused. "We both know you'd be able to perform playing either instrument after practicing a couple of hours."

"With a wife and two kids, I don't have a couple of hours to practice."

"I heard you've planned Sparky's bachelor party for the VFW. That should be quite an evening. Word is that the Vietnam veterans are excited about the stripper."

"There won't be a stripper."

"Too bad," Brian replied. "That would've really upped the sales of meat raffle tickets. Dean Weske told me they were hoping to raise enough money to buy an electric scooter for one of the guys in the veterans' home."

"I'm sorry. Tell Dean he'll have to come up with another scheme to sell more tickets."

"If you were a team player..."

I raised my hand to stop Brian. "There isn't going to be a stripper at the VFW bachelor party. The discussion is over."

"You're certain?"

"I'm absolutely, one hundred percent sure there will *NOT* be a stripper at the VFW. Tell Dean he can hire his own stripper for a different night if he thinks that'll draw a bigger crowd."

"Dang!" Brian said, snapping his fingers. "I'd even dreamt up an excuse to slip out of the house."

"You already told me there was a band practice."

"There you go! A perfect alibi, wasted."

After Brian left, I locked away the original map. With a copy spread on my desktop, I called Kerry. "What's up, sailor?" he asked.

"I just sent you an email. The attachment is a copy of the map I found inside the puzzle box."

"What am I supposed to do with it? Do you expect me to go out and dig up the buried treasure?"

I heard computer keys clacking as Kerry pulled up his email. "No, I just want to have copies out in the computer cloud in case someone steals the original."

"Why don't you just go out and dig up the treasure?" Kerry asked.

"First of all, I don't know where this map begins. Secondly, I don't know that there's a treasure. Thirdly, I'm not sure it's buried."

"That's certainly depressing. How are you going to answer those questions?"

"I don't know if I can answer them. The starting point appears to be a crazy Norwegian's place."

Kerry chuckled. "In military terms, that's a target-rich environment. Most of the locals think a lot of Norwegians are crazy just for eating lutefisk."

"I just spoke with Brian Johnson. He suggested that 'Crazy' might be a person's nickname."

"Okay. Who would that be?"

"He didn't know of anyone who went by that nickname."

Kerry laughed. "I know where you could find a hundred people with knowledge of historical nicknames."

Sighing, I replied, "Yeah, I'll ask the residents." Seeing the clock, I froze. "I've got to run. Catch you later."

"Ah, the VFW bachelor party is coming up."

"Are you planning to be there?"

Kerry chuckled. "The attendance of the police chief would probably be unwelcome."

* * *

Driving home, the question of identifying the *crazy Norwegian's place* swirled in my brain. I pulled ahead to Highway 61, prepared to turn south when Kerry's comment about finding an expert struck gold. I changed my turn signal and went north toward Silver Bay. Driving toward town, I proceeded up the hill until I saw the library sign.

When I walked in, the librarian was sorting through a stack of returned books. She looked up and smiled. "How can I help you, Peter?"

Surprised that Shannon would remember me from our field trip to Silver Bay, I composed my thoughts. "I need local information. I have a treasure map, but I don't know the starting point."

Shannon smiled and leaned on the counter. "Tell me more."

I unfolded a copy of the map and spread it between us. "I have this spot that says, 'crazy Norwegian's place.' I have no idea what or where that is. Can you help me?"

"Do you think it's somewhere local?"

"The map was inside a piano donated to Whistling Pines by a Two Harbors resident. I assume it's something her husband, a local antique dealer, drew up."

"Nothing comes to mind, but if I can make a copy of this, I'll give it some thought."

"If you promise not to search for the hidden treasure without me, you can make a copy."

Shannon laughed and took the map to a copier. "Do you know what the hidden treasure is?" she asked as the machine scanned, then fed out a copy.

"I have no idea whatsoever."

"But it could be worth millions?" she asked.

Folding the map and returning it to my pocket, I replied, "Sure."

Reading my body language, Shannon smiled. "Thousands?"

"Let's focus on the entertainment value of the hunt," I suggested.

"Would you mind if I contacted Madeline at the Two Harbors Library? She might have some different resources related to that immediate area and south to Duluth."

"The more the merrier!" I replied.

Shannon glanced at the pile of books she'd been sorting, then sighed. "I may prioritize a treasure hunt over returning books to the shelves."

"The map is old and yellowed. If the treasure is still there, and I'm not sure it is, there's no rush to discover it right away."

"Work with me, Peter," Shannon said. "This sounds like the most interesting thing I've had to do in..."

"In how long?"

Shannon leaned close and whispered, "Sadly, I can't think of anything I've *ever* done as a librarian that's more interesting than this. Give me your phone number. I'll call you when I have something."

I returned to my car, hoping I wasn't wasting her time.

I had just passed Beaver Bay when my phone rang. Using Bluetooth, I answered as I drove without seeing who was calling. "This is Peter."

"Hi, Peter. This is Shannon."

"Did I forget something at the library?" I asked.

"No, but I have information for you."

"Really? Already?"

"I found a reference to an old hotel operated by an alcoholic Norwegian that housed a lot of immigrants when they first arrived here. The history books refer to him as foolish, which the thesaurus lists as an alternative to crazy. I also spoke with Madeline. She suggested the fishing piers and fish houses constructed by the Norwegian fishermen. She said a lot of them were considered crazy because they were out on Lake Superior fishing in all kinds of bad weather."

"Wow, that's a lot."

"What are you doing first thing tomorrow morning?"

Momentarily thrown off by the quick change in the conversation, I paused for a moment, and then said, "I usually go to Whistling Pines. Why?"

"Could you meet Madeline and me at the Two Harbors Library? We'll show you what we've discovered."

"There's really not that big of a rush."

"Peter, humor us. We find this diversion interesting and fun."

"What time does the library open?"

"We'll meet you at nine o'clock."

* * *

162

Arriving at home later than usual, I found Jenny and the children already eating supper. The remains of a grocery store rotisserie chicken lay on the cutting board alongside the stove, where two pots sat with spoons sticking out.

"Get yourself a plate of chicken," Jenny called from the dining room. "The potatoes and green beans on the stove should still be warm."

Loading my plate, I joined the family at the table as Jeremy squirmed. Having finished his meal, he was awaiting permission to clear his plate and move on to television. "Can I be excused?" he asked.

"May I be excused," I corrected.

Jeremy frowned. "You haven't eaten anything. Why do you want to be excused?"

Ignoring Jenny's chuckle, I said, "I was correcting you. *May I be excused?* is the proper way to request permission to leave the table. *Can I be excused?* is asking if you're physically able to be excused."

"I don't understand the difference," he replied.

Wishing to eat and not debate, I said, "Just use *may* instead of *can* when you ask to be excused from the table."

"Fine. May I be excused?"

"You may, if you'll clear your plate and glass."

As he disappeared into the kitchen, Jenny leaned until our shoulders touched.

"Who knew parenting would be so challenging?"

"The scary thing is this may be one of the easier parts. We're not into girls, cars, dating, alcohol, and curfews yet."

Feeling ignored, Amy hurled a green bean that hit Jenny in the face.

Wiping her face with a napkin, Jenny turned to Amy and said, "We don't throw food."

"I found out who broke into my office," I said as Jenny cleaned up Amy and her highchair.

"Someone admitted breaking in?"

"Not in so many words. But the dentist danced around the break-in issue, and he was too interested in the location and contents of the puzzle box."

"Did you tell Kerry?"

"I'll tell him, but there's nothing to be done about it. Nothing was stolen, and Kerry never checked for fingerprints or other evidence at the scene."

"I suppose he has bigger fish to fry."

"I had a very interesting discussion with Shannon, the Silver Bay Librarian. She's researching possible locations that might be called *the crazy Norwegian's place*."

"Does she have time to do something like that?"

"Shannon was excited about being part of a real-life treasure hunt. She called as I was driving home with some information. She's enlisted Madeline from the Two Harbors

Library, too. We're meeting tomorrow morning to look over what they've found."

"They've already found something?"

"There are a couple of locations that might be 'the crazy Norwegian's place.'"

"Do you really believe there's something there?"

"I wasn't sure until I met the dentist. He's too interested in finding the box for the map to lead us nowhere."

"What's your best guess about the so-called treasure?"

"Astrid's husband was an antique dealer. Maybe he acquired a piece of stolen property and stashed it, hoping to sell it at a substantial profit later."

"Like jewelry?"

"Or maybe a book or painting. Who knows?"

"If this is really buried treasure, it must be something that would survive underground for decades."

"A cache of gems?"

Jenny snorted as she lifted Amy from the highchair. "No one around here has money to buy a bunch of diamonds or gems. The local folks have barely eked out a living for a hundred years. The prosperous people had good jobs with the mining companies or the railroads."

"How about the fishermen?"

"Like I said, the prosperous people worked for the mines or the railroad. Most of the commercial fishermen went broke or died as paupers."

"Maybe someone inherited the Romanov jewels!" I joked.

"Sure. I doubt any Finnish logger had millions of dollars' worth of jewels and chose to continue his subsistence life just so his wealth wouldn't be too evident."

"You know that Kerry accused me of being sarcastic."

With Amy on her hip, Jenny smiled, guessing what Kerry had actually said. "I suppose his comment involved the word for a wise donkey."

"What's the other word for a wise donkey?" Jeremy asked from the other room.

Jenny shook her head. "Yet he never hears me ask about his homework." Setting Amy on the floor, Jenny asked, "What time are you meeting the librarians?"

"The library opens at nine o'clock. Shannon said to meet them then."

"She must be really excited if she's driving down from Silver Bay to meet with you when the library opens. You'd better bring them coffee and doughnuts."

"I thought women shunned high-calorie foods like doughnuts."

Jenny sighed. "Bringing doughnuts is a universal show of goodwill. Even if they choose not to eat them, they'll be pleased that you appreciated their help enough to bring treats."

A knock on the back door interrupted our discussion. Wiping my fingers on a paper napkin as I walked to the door, I was surprised to find Sparky standing there.

"Have you got a minute?"

"What's up?"

"Wendy says that I'm socially immature."

Thinking Wendy's opinion was spot on, I replied, "Is that a problem?"

"I've always thought I was reasonably smart. I mean, I can reason through a computer or fire truck pump problem. That's maturity, isn't it?"

"You're confusing school smart with social awareness."

"I don't understand."

"You might be a computer wizard, but you struggled with dating Wendy. Did your conversations lag?"

"Not usually. I mean, Wendy has a lot to say about many topics."

"What did you lend to those conversations?"

"I didn't have to talk much at all. You know, Wendy can hold both sides of a conversation. Mostly, I smiled and nodded."

"Did she ever ask you about your life and values?"

The question seemed to stump Sparky. "I guess we must've talked about the fire department and me being the chief."

"Did you ever take her to a movie?"

"Yeah, we went to a couple of movies."

"Did you discuss the choices and agree on one you both wanted to see?"

"I was happy to see whatever Wendy wanted to see."

"Did you discuss which music you liked on the car radio?"

"Wendy likes the country music station out of Duluth. She can sing along with every song."

"What *did* you discuss?"

"We talked about places we could be alone." Sparky paused. "And she asked me to set up her wireless printer so it connected with her computer."

"Have you ever talked about politics or social issues?"

"Not that I can recall."

"It sounds like Wendy has been the driving force in your relationship."

Sparky nodded. "I suppose so. It's not like I wanted to go any different direction than she suggested."

"What do you discuss with the firemen?"

"Fire trucks, fire calls, hunting..." Sparky stalled at three topics.

"Have you ever had a conversation with Stella Hygge?"

Sparky frowned as he thought. "I set her up with some classes when she first joined the department."

"Have you ever discussed your mother with her?"

"Why would I do that? What does Stella care about Mom?"

"Have you ever had a discussion with a woman other than your mother or Wendy?"

"Sure. I've asked Jenny how to deal with Wendy."

"I mean a philosophical discussion." Seeing Sparky's lost look, I expanded. "Have you talked about your views about the community, politics, or even the weather?"

"Sure. People complain about the weather all the time. I generally agree with them."

"Do you usually vote for Democratic or Republican candidates?"

"Mom says there hasn't been an honest politician since Eisenhower. I usually skip the elections unless there's a pro-fire department candidate. They always get my vote."

Taking Sparky's elbow, I steered him toward the door. "I suggest you pull up CNN to see what topic is hot. Listen to their discussion, then strike up a conversation with someone tomorrow about that subject."

"Most people I talk to want their computer fixed. They're not much interested in anything else."

"Fine. Go to Judy's for lunch and talk to someone at the lunch counter about politics."

Sparky stopped on the back step. "I usually eat a sandwich at my computer."

"Try something new. Get out of your rut."

"But Peter, I don't like to talk to strangers."

"Like I said, get out of your rut. Step outside of the house. Try something new."

I closed the door and leaned against it. Jenny walked into the kitchen, looking smug. "Wendy's right, Sparky is socially immature."

"I think immature would be a step up. I think he's socially handicapped."

"But he handled the news people so well during the art studio protest."

"Maybe that's it! He blossoms when he's acting as the fire chief."

Jenny nodded and smiled. "So, he knows how to interact with people. He just chooses not to. He's a classic introvert."

"Which is why he and Wendy get along so well. They balance each other."

"Yin and yang," Jenny said. "Wendy talks, and Sparky listens."

Chapter 12

I found Shannon and Madeline in a small room just inside the Two Harbors Library entrance. I set a carrier with four Styrofoam cups, sugar, creamer, and a bag of pastries on the table. "Would you two like a cup of coffee and a doughnut or roll?"

Smiling, Shannon took a cup of coffee from the carrier. Madeline peeked in the bag of goodies. "Would you mind if I took just half the chocolate iced doughnut?"

"Help yourself to whatever you'd like."

After carefully lifting her doughnut with a napkin, Madeline handed the bag to Shannon. She looked into the bag, then looked at me with a smile. I realized Jenny was correct. The two librarians deeply appreciated the gesture of bringing goodies as thanks for their help.

Shannon and Madeline had obviously been setting up for me well in advance of my arrival. The table was spread with maps and historical books.

Madeline handed me what appeared to be a very old book with the title *A History of the North Shore.* "I bookmarked the page about the Norwegian Hotel. A lot of new

Norwegian immigrants lived there while looking for jobs. The owner was a tight-fisted woman with a wandering eye. Some people called her Wall-Eyed-Mary. Others said she was Crazy Mary. As the flow of immigrants slowed, Mary turned the hotel into a boarding house. After her death, the boarding house was purchased by a large family.”

Shannon continued, “I thought that hotel might be ‘the crazy Norwegian’s place.’” Moving to a plat map, she pointed to a lot. “Based on your map, the treasure is buried thirty undefined units away from the corner of whatever that place is. Depending on the direction you went, thirty yards would put the treasure under the house built behind the old hotel or even under the street.”

Madeline wrinkled her nose. “If that was the case, the treasure might have been either buried deeper and paved over, or it was probably discovered when they dug the foundation for the neighboring house.”

After wiping the icing from her fingers, Shannon gestured to a book open to a picture of a weathered wooden shack perched above Lake Superior. “Back in the days of big-time commercial fishing, every fisherman had a pier and fish house. They stowed their gear and cleaned their catch in their fish houses, like this one.”

“Okay, what’s the significance?” I asked.

Sliding a map in front of me, Madeline pointed to a series of “X” marks running up the shoreline from Duluth to beyond Silver Bay. "As near as I can tell from the records and from pictures Shannon found, each of these marks is the approximate location of a pier and fish house."

"There were this many commercial fishermen here?" I asked.

Madeline nodded. "Not all of them were active at the same time, but yes, over the years, there were dozens of private piers and fish houses."

"Are any of them still there?" I asked.

Shannon pulled over a coffee table book and opened it to pages she'd marked with Post-it flags. "These photos were taken by Mac Jacobson, a local photographer who specializes in old barns, outhouses, and mining shacks. He's located the remnants of a dozen or more of the old piers and fish shacks."

"Wow. This is great, but I'm not sure we'll be able to identify a specific location from the map found in the puzzle box. It just says, 'Crazy Norwegian's place.' I don't know if it's meant to describe a business, farm, house, or something else."

Shannon replied, "A lot of the Norwegian immigrants had fished for North Sea herring. They slid right into fishing the Lake Superior freshwater herring."

Trying to be politely skeptical, I said, "But how do we determine which might have belonged to a 'Crazy Norwegian?'"

Setting aside the photo book, Shannon pulled over a different, dog-eared volume and opened it to a marked tab. "Here's a list of fishing companies from the early twentieth century." Halfway down the page, she put her finger on a listing. "The Gal Norske Fish Company had a pier near Beaver Bay."

Frowning, I said, "I'm not looking for a female Norwegian fishing company."

Shaking her head, Shannon took out her cell phone and said, "Siri, what's the Norwegian word for crazy?"

After a pause, Siri responded, "The Norwegian word for crazy is 'gal.'"

Smiling, Shannon asked, "Siri, how do you say crazy Norwegian in Norway?"

"A crazy Norwegian would be called a 'gal Norske.'"

Going back to the maps, Madeline pointed to an X which she circled with a red pen. "Here! The Gal Norske Fish Company. It's the crazy Norwegian Fish Company's pier and fish shack."

I leaned back to process all the information I'd just learned. Shannon and Madeline stared at me expectantly. "Well?"

"I could hug both of you," I said.

Shannon slid her chair away from me. "That's not the normal response for information retrieval."

Madeline laughed nervously.

Realizing I'd embarrassed them, I said, "Sorry. It's a figure of speech."

"Have we found the starting point of your treasure map?" Madeline asked.

"I'll call the police chief, and we'll go out with a metal detector."

Shannon stood and gathered up the books she'd consulted. Madeline stopped halfway through folding the map and looked at me. "Is this a hunt for an honest-to-god buried treasure?"

"We think so."

Madeline bit her lower lip as if considering her next words. "Can I come with you? I mean, this would be epic."

Shannon's eyes brightened. "I'd like to be part of this, too."

Looking at their professional attire I said, "You two don't get out of the libraries much, do you?"

Shannon laughed. "I'm a librarian. No, I don't get away much. And never for a treasure hunt."

"Change into jeans and boots and bring shovels. I'll meet you ladies in Beaver Bay two hours from now."

The librarians' eyes went wide. "Really?"

"You're now part of the search team."

Tucking a stack of books under her arm, Shannon said, "I've got to call the city manager. We'll need my assistant to cover for me."

Madeline finished folding the map and said, "I'll just lock the library and put out a closed sign."

Shannon laughed. "You're terrible. I'll find someone for library coverage and see you in two hours."

I called Kerry from my car. "I may have located the starting point for the puzzle box map."

"You found a crazy Norwegian?" he asked, chuckling.

"The Two Harbors and Silver Bay librarians found the Crazy Norwegian Fishing Company pier and fish house near Beaver Bay."

"Seriously?"

"The title is in Norwegian, but yes, it's the actual name of a company. Grab your metal detector and meet me in Beaver Bay two hours from now. The two librarians will meet us there."

"Beaver Bay is outside my jurisdiction. I'll notify the sheriff's department."

"Do you think they'll send a deputy or want the BCA to be involved?"

Kerry paused. "Peter, this sounds crazy and stupid to me. I can't imagine what the sheriff, who hasn't been part of this whole insane scenario, will say. I'm certain that he won't feel the need to have any of his officers involved in a treasure hunt based on a map found in an old piano."

"Why don't you call Kevin, the conservation officer? He's been up for our other adventures."

"I'll tell you what I'll do. I'm going to call Pastor Olafson and he can contact the entire poker group to see who might be interested in a hopeless treasure hunt.”

“It sounds stupid when you say it like that.”

“Peter, it is stupid! What odds would you put on us finding a *treasure* based on an old map with an obscure starting point and no idea what treasure we’re looking for? I’m betting that anything valuable would’ve been removed decades ago, even if it was buried at the location on the map.”

“We need to look,” I said. “Besides, the two librarians are excited.”

“Oh, gee. If the librarians are excited, we’d better jump on it.”

“Your sarcasm is wasted on me.”

“Think about what you said. ‘The librarians are excited.’ That’s a pretty low threshold. How much does it take to excite a librarian who spends her days shushing people?”

“They worked hard on this and deserve credit for coming up with the Norwegian translation and location.”

“I apologize. I’ll call Ron Olafson to see if he can round up any of the group. I’ll be in Beaver Bay with whoever is available.”

“Thank you.”

“Peter, you never answered my question. What are the odds of actually finding something?”

“Maybe ten percent.”

“I think you’re overly optimistic.”

"Do you have something more interesting or pressing to do?"

"This treasure hunt isn't even on my radar. Stopping a speeder would be a higher priority than this."

"Fine. Let me borrow the metal detector."

"No. No. I'll be there, and I'll smile."

Chapter 13

Three pickups and three cars were parked in front of the Beaver Bay strip mall, with seven people milling around. The unlikely crew included the police chief, two librarians, a conservation officer, a Lutheran pastor, a former Marine/farmer, and me.

Madeline spread a map on the conservation officer's pickup hood. Pointing to a red-circled X, she said, "This is where the Gal Norwegian Fishing Company pier was located. Shannon found a picture of their fishing shack in a coffee table book."

Shannon offered a printed copy of the picture, which showed the collapsed and weather-beaten remnants of the wooden building, now overgrown with aspen and evergreens. "This is the photo of the Gal Norwegian fish house from Mac Jacobson's book."

Kevin, the conservation officer shook his head. "I've been in that area. It's thick."

Kerry nodded to me. "Show them your map."

I spread a copy of the map on the pickup's hood. "The writing is hard to decipher, but it appears to show a point here, with the note, 'crazy Norwegian's place,' and then a dotted line with '30' written on the dots."

Pastor Olafson put on his reading glasses and leaned close. "Are you sure that's 30 and not 50?"

"Yeah, that's a little hard to read, isn't it. Let's assume it's 30. If we don't find anything at 30 yards, we can look at 50."

Augie, the former Marine, scratched his head. "I've followed some crazy handwritten maps, but this one is terrible. Which direction does that line go from the starting point? It goes up and to the left. Do you think that means we're going northwest from the corner of the fish house?"

"That's my assumption," I replied.

"I've got another question," Augie said, picking up my map. "It says, '30'. Thirty what? Steps? Feet? Yards?"

Shannon, who'd been standing back listening, said, "Maybe the guy was an ocean fisherman, and the measurement is fathoms!"

Madeline sniffed, hiding her laugh. "I just read an article about the Harvard Bridge. An engineering student measured it in 'Smoots,' which was his height. The bridge is marked in ten Smoot increments."

Pastor Olafson's smile broadened. "Maybe it's 30 cubits, like Noah's Ark."

Stopping the joking, I said, "Let's assume the map maker didn't have a ruler along and buried the treasure thirty paces northwest from the corner."

Kevin nodded and removed the map from the hood of his pickup. "I'm familiar with this area. We have to drive down a path cut through the timber. I think you should all climb in the four-wheel-drive pickups with Augie and me."

Shannon grabbed my elbow and urged me toward the backseat of Kevin's pickup. "This is exciting!"

"What did the city administrator say when you told her you were going on a treasure hunt?"

"Lana wanted to join us."

"She was welcome to come along," I said as I climbed into the truck beside Madeline, who was nearly bouncing with excitement.

Madeline smiled, raising a brow. "I got one of the library board people to cover for me. I was a little worried when he showed up with his tuba."

I closed my eyes, picturing Brian walking into the library with his tuba. "Your board member is Brian Johnson?"

Madeline nodded. "I told him he couldn't play his tuba in the library. He pointed out there was no one else in the building. Then he asked, 'if a tuba plays in the library and there's no one there to hear it, has it made a sound?'"

"That sounds like Brian."

We all sat quietly as Kevin drove out of Beaver Bay and then turned down a gravel road. We'd only driven a quarter mile when he turned onto a path that was little more than two muddy ruts overgrown with grass. The ruts followed a narrow opening in the underbrush for nearly half a mile. Stopping in the ruts with no obvious landmarks, Kevin turned to us. "If I'm not mistaken, the fish shack is about fifty yards from here."

Walking single-file through the underbrush, we followed Kevin through the narrow gaps that were apparently a game trail. The forest was lush, and the pine scent became intense when Kevin pushed aside small balsam branches, allowing us to pass. The fresh aroma of lake air preceded our emergence from the underbrush into a small opening overlooking Lake Superior. Below us was a small beach with a few leaning posts, bent by shifting ice and pounding waves. A few boards littered the shore above the beach. I assumed this was once a fisherman's pier.

Alongside the opening was a mostly collapsed structure that showed signs of having once been painted white. The remaining boards had been bleached by sunlight and rain into a silverish tan. The roof had collapsed, and all the walls leaned away from the lake, thanks to high waves and decades of wind.

Kevin put headphones over his cap and activated the metal detector. He waved the circular end over the rusty door hinges, causing a whooping sound, audible to those of us standing near him. Kerry turned his own metal detector on and repeated the exercise.

Kevin gestured for me to lead. "Lead us to the treasure, Doc."

I led the group around fallen boards and encroaching trees to what I estimated was the northwest corner of the fish house. Looking in the direction I thought we should go, I realized my direct path was blocked by small trees and a fallen pine.

Augie patted me on the shoulder. "Take one step directly aside, then keep counting your forward steps until you can step back onto your direct trail."

"Thanks," I replied as I started counting my paces away from the fish house.

Kerry, Pastor Olafson, and Shannon, who was wearing gardening gloves and carrying a spade, took a parallel path a few feet to our right.

When I'd counted thirty paces, I stopped and gestured to the spot. Kevin stepped forward and waved the metal detector over the spot I'd indicated. "Nothing," he said, as Madeline watched, ready to dig if we identified anything.

Augie, who had a prosthetic leg, stepped past me. "You weren't taking full strides, Peter. I think we need to continue a bit farther."

Kevin followed Augie, sweeping the metal detector side to side as he walked.

When Augie stopped, Kevin swept the immediate area, but found nothing.

I looked to my right but couldn't see Kerry's group. "Shannon!"

Her voice came from somewhere in the underbrush. "We found a bunch of tin cans."

"I suppose that's one kind of treasure," Augie said, smirking.

"Let's move over a couple of feet and backtrack," Kevin suggested, stepping to his left and sweeping the metal detector as he moved.

Augie sidled up to Madeline. In a stage whisper meant to be heard by the rest of us, he said, "Peter *thinks* that line is drawn to the northwest. There were no directional markings to indicate which way is up."

Madeline nodded and replied, "Who's to say we should be looking thirty paces away from the building. Maybe we should be thirty Smoots out."

Augie patted her shoulder. "I like you. Where's the library?"

"What? You've never been to the library?"

"I get my news and information off the internet," Augie replied as we stepped around a soggy spot in the underbrush.

"The library has more to offer, and my sources are less...questionable than the internet information."

Augie listened to Madeline's take on the internet, then asked for directions to the Two Harbors Library. Kevin had started a new line, searching farther west a bit from our previous two paths.

"We've got something!" Ron Olafson called from somewhere east of us.

Madeline looked at me and asked, "Should we go over there?"

Shaking my head, I replied, "Let them make sure it's not another pile of tin cans before we get excited."

Kevin stopped abruptly and focused his sweeps on a small area, causing his headphones to whoop. "Madeline, bring your shovel."

Trudging ahead through a mucky area, she passed Augie and approached Kevin. Digging where Kevin gestured, she scooped moist ground from the spot. Kevin swung his hoop over each scoop of dirt to check for metal. The fourth scoop stopped him. "Break up that clump of dirt," he ordered.

She poked at the dirt with the tip of her spade, spreading the pile on the forest floor. Her shovel hit something, making a metallic clinking sound. Excited, Madeline set the shovel aside. Dropping to her knees, she pulled apart the dirt until she held up a small disk.

Augie squatted next to her. "It's a button." He looked up at me. "Is this a treasure?"

"I doubt it. Who would draw a detailed map to a place where they'd hidden a button?"

"It's here!" Shannon shouted from somewhere east of us. "We've got something!"

Madeline stood and grabbed her shovel and then we slogged through the swampy forest toward the voices. Shannon's voice was more animated and carried farther through the underbrush. After a few minutes of walking, we found Shannon and Pastor Olafson on hands and knees clawing at the dirt while Kerry watched. Hearing us approach, Kerry looked our way and smiled.

Shannon and the pastor dug at the ground like two dogs uncovering a bone. Getting closer, I could see they were removing the dirt packed around a rectangular box with a rusty metal handle on one end. The box appeared to be olive green, and the paint seemed to have preserved the box from the moist ground. Excited by the find, Madeline got down on her hands and knees to help Shannon and Pastor Olafson remove the dirt surrounding the box.

Kerry leaned close to me. "I'll be darned. There really was a treasure box buried out here."

"Oh, ye of little faith."

"What can I say? Cops are skeptical cynics."

"I've got my fingers under the edge," Madeline announced.

"Lift it gently," Olafson said.

The box, which appeared to be almost three feet long and more than a foot wide, was slowly wrestled out of the hole. Apparently, it was heavy, with the librarians and pastor struggling to lift it free from the hole. Setting the box on top of the muck they'd dug out, the three of them sat back and brushed the dirt from their gloves.

"Huh," Kerry said. "That's an army footlocker."

Brushing back loose hair that had fallen out of her cap, Shannon asked, "What do you think is inside it?"

Chuckling, because Shannon's move had smeared mud across her cheek and forehead, Pastor Olafson asked, "I don't suppose the key was inside the box with the map?"

"There wasn't a key," I replied.

"Can we use a shovel to pry the lock open?" Madeline asked.

Kerry stepped forward. "I'd rather open it in a more controlled location. If it's not too heavy, can Ron and Augie carry it to one of the pickups? We'll take it into Two Harbors, clean the dirt off, and open it in the police department garage."

Wiping the dirt from her jeans, Madeline said, "Let's call the newspaper and have them take pictures when we open the box. It might be like a time capsule."

"Maybe it's full of money!" Shannon said, following Augie and the pastor as they lifted the box by its rusty handles and walked toward the fish house.

Kerry looked at me. "What's your guess?"

"Something from Korea."

Kerry grimaced. "Let's hope it's not something the owner was hoping to dispose of."

"Like what?" Kevin asked.

"Worst case?" Kerry asked.

"Sure. What's the worst case?" I asked.

"The box is filled with hand grenades."

"It's not that heavy," Augie said over his shoulder. "I've lugged boxes of grenades and ammo. They're heavier than this. Dynamite and C4 explosives are lighter."

"That'd be so much better," Kerry replied sarcastically. "We'd have to get the bomb squad from the Twin Cities to deal with that."

"Let's get the box open before we get too excited," I said.

* * *

The two librarians, Kevin, and I speculated on the foot locker's contents as he drove to Two Harbors. Arriving at the police station, Kerry opened the garage door while Augie and I set up a folding table. Shannon found a roll of paper towels and wiped dirt off the footlocker while Ron Olafson examined the lock.

"I assume you have a crowbar, Chief," the pastor said, standing back.

Augie, who was as strong as an ox, stepped up to the box. He wrapped one of his big hands around the lock and twisted, ripping free the screws securing the hasp.

Stepping back, he looked at us, who were in awe of his strength and simple solution to opening the box. "Well, who's going to open it?" he asked.

I gestured toward the table and said, "Madeline and Shannon identified the secret location. I think they should have the honor of opening our treasure trunk."

The two women were almost giddy. Stepping forward, they jointly lifted the lid making the rusty hinges groan. "Something's wrapped in fabric," Shannon said.

Kerry pulled rubber gloves from his pocket and handed a pair to each of the women. "Use these."

Accepting the gloves, Shannon asked, "Are these to protect the treasure from our fingerprints or to protect us from dirt and germs?"

Kerry raised his unscarred eyebrow. "Maybe both."

After donning the gloves, Madeline lifted a corner of the wrapper, then gasped. "This fabric is silk, and it's wrapped around something gold."

"With inlaid jade," Shannon added.

We crowded around the table to look at what was apparently a crown.

"Holy lutefisk," Ron Olafson said. "I've seen pictures of crowns like this. It must be worth millions."

Carefully lifting the crown from the box, Shannon turned it so we could see it from all sides. "It's beautiful. It appears to be oriental."

"Astrid's husband reportedly shipped treasures home from Korea," I said.

"I don't quite know how to deal with this," Kerry confessed. "I need to contact the State Department, who will have to involve someone from the Korean embassy."

Augie peeked inside the box. "There's something else in here."

Picking up a smaller silk-wrapped piece, Augie carefully folded back the silk. "It's like a miniature samurai sword made from white jade."

Turning it while cradling it in the silk wrapping, Augie seemed awestruck...until he froze. "Kerry, this rust-colored stain on the silk might be blood."

Kerry stepped closer and examined the fabric. "Put it back into the box, Augie. I'll call the BCA and ask for forensic assistance." He nodded to Shannon. "Put it all back in the box. We need to secure these items."

Shannon gently placed the crown back in the box, then stepped back. Taking a breath while staring at the box, she smiled. "Wow! There really was a treasure."

Madeline stepped over to me and grasped my arm. "Thanks for including us, Peter. This is the most exciting thing that's happened since I went to the American Library Association conference in Memphis!"

Shannon started laughing. "You obviously had more fun at the convention than I did. This is *way more* exciting than any library convention!"

A car pulled up outside of the garage, and a young redheaded woman scrambled out. Steph, the reporter from *The Harbor View* newspaper, rushed into the garage. "Madeline, where's the treasure?"

Madeline nodded toward the footlocker sitting on the table. "It's there, Steph."

Raising her iPad, Steph took a photo of the box. "What's inside?"

Kerry stepped between the reporter and the box. "Steph, there's something very valuable inside the box. Until I get it examined and secured, you can't write about this in the paper."

"No problem," Steph said, craning her neck to look past Kerry. "The paper doesn't come out until next Thursday. What's in the box?"

"A gold crown and a miniature jade samurai sword," Madeline said.

Steph started typing into her iPad. "Are they worth a lot?"

Pastor Olafson shook his head. "They're not worth *a lot*. They're probably invaluable. I've never seen a nephrite dagger before."

"Nephrite?" I asked.

"It's a rare form of white jade," Olafson replied.

Stephanie froze. "Who do they belong to?"

Kerry stared at the box. "Probably the people of Korea. We'll have to get the State Department involved to make that determination."

"Whoa!" Steph said, continuing to type into her iPad. "Is there a finder's fee?"

"I suppose that'll be up to the Korean government to decide."

I nodded. "These are probably among the tens of thousands of artifacts stolen during the Korean War."

Augie edged close to Kerry and whispered, "I wonder how old that blood stain is?"

Kerry nodded. "Me too."

Walking toward Shannon, who was standing on the other side of the table, I whispered, "Can you check the newspaper archives for an unsolved stabbing in the 1950s?"

Her eyes went wide when she reasoned through finding the bloody dagger and Augie's question to Kerry. "Wow. Sure."

* * *

My cell phone chirped, signaling an incoming call. "Jenny's calling. I'll catch you later."

"You're running late, dear. I fed the kids without you."

Catching the edge in my wife's voice, I replied, "Did you save some for me?"

"There's leftover roasted chicken, green bean hotdish, and mashed potatoes in the refrigerator."

Kicking myself for losing track of time, I said, "I'm sorry. I'll grab a bite, then run off to the VFW for Sparky's party."

"Wendy just left. She wanted to make sure there wasn't going to be a stripper at the VFW. I assured her there were no naked women invited to the party. That's true, correct?"

"There won't be any naked women at the VFW tonight."

Jenny ended the call, and as I walked to my car I thought, *no naked women unless the firemen have something planned.*

Chapter 14

After apologizing for missing supper and wolfing down a chicken breast and a scoop of mashed potatoes, I walked next door to fetch Sparky. He met me at the door looking terrified. The armpits of his dark blue Two Harbors Fire Department t-shirt were sweat-stained. "I'm not sure I can do this," he said, pacing up and down the hallway.

"You're a fireman. You're tough. The bachelor party is no big deal. Just sit back, watch the meat raffle, and let people buy you drinks. I'll be your sober driver, so you don't have to worry about getting a DWI."

"It's not that, Doc. I don't know if I'm ready for this whole marriage and parent thing. It's like I was a kid only yesterday. Now, I'm supposed to be a responsible adult with a wife and kid."

"Everyone has stage fright before their wedding. It's perfectly normal."

"You had second thoughts?"

I took Sparky's elbow and led him outside. "I didn't have second thoughts as much as a fear of not being prepared for stepping into the role of husband and father."

"That's right. You stepped into a ready-made family with Jeremy already a part of the picture."

"He was really good about it. We had a serious man-to-man talk. I assured him I wanted to be his dad. I asked if he was willing to accept that."

Sparky got into my car, then asked, "What did he say?"

"He was a little taken aback that I was asking the question. He assumed that whatever happened was between Jenny and me. I think he was touched to be asked if he was ready to be a part of the relationship."

"Did he say yes?"

"As I recall, he just hugged me. I don't know if he ever verbalized his reply."

"That's pretty cool," Sparky said before frowning. "How do you think that will go with a baby? I've never dealt with an infant before."

"Amy's arrival was all new territory for me, too. There were sleepless nights and tension as we redefined our relationships, but all four of us got through it. I think the greatest adjustment may have been on Jeremy's part. He was accustomed to being an only child. He felt like he'd been bumped off our priority list. A baby's needs always take precedence. That sometimes meant that Jeremy had to wait for us to deal with Amy's needs before helping him. In the end, it all worked out. I think he takes pride in being a big brother now." I realized Sparky was staring at me without speaking. "What's wrong? Did you forget something?"

"A second kid? I haven't adjusted to the idea of a first kid yet. Are you saying there could be two?"

"That's up to you and Wendy. It's not a decision you'll have to make immediately."

"What if Wendy has twins? There could be two kids right away!"

"The doctor would've noticed two heartbeats and seen two babies on the ultrasounds. There's virtually no chance Wendy would be having twins without her knowing it before now."

Sparky relaxed. "Okay. Good."

* * *

I led Sparky into the VFW, where a couple of dozen Vietnam vets and their wives were seated at tables. A whoop from the bar turned my focus to the five firemen wearing dark blue uniforms, seated on bar stools. Stella Hygge shrugged like she'd already lost control of the group.

Vern pointed to three round tables he'd arranged in the back recess of the bar. "Take your rowdy friends over there so they don't disrupt my regular customers."

As Stella and I herded firemen from the bar to the round tables, two men entered carrying a white and red cooler between them. Behind the men, three women in VFW logo sweatshirts walked in. One carried a roll of tickets. The others carried a bingo tumbler with a hand crank. Vern directed them to two long tables arranged against a wall in the opposite corner from the firemen.

Finishing off his beverage, one of the firemen held up his mug and yelled, "Hey, Vern, can you bring a couple of pitchers and more mugs?"

Vern nodded and started filling a pitcher from a tap behind the bar.

As Sparky mingled with the firemen, I edged over to Stella, who was drinking clear liquid. "What's your beverage of choice?"

She held up the glass and smiled, "Fizzy water with a lime."

I relaxed, realizing that the boring bachelor party just might materialize. "Thanks. Will you be able to keep these rowdies under control?"

Stella looked toward the firemen, at least two of them already showing the effects of the beer. "I think so. In an hour, they'll be past the point of causing trouble." She nodded toward my guitar case. "Are you going to carry that around all night or are you actually going to play a song?"

Setting the guitar case on a tabletop, I asked, "What would you like to hear?"

"I'm partial to country. How about something by Garth Brooks."

After tuning the guitar, I waited for Vern to deliver the pitchers, then strummed a few chords before singing, "Blame it all on my roots. I showed up in boots and ruined your black-tie affair..."

The chatter died out as people turned to listen to me sing, "Friends in Low Places." A few voices joined me in the chorus, and even the half-drunk firemen were distracted from needling Sparky. Playing the chords from memory, I was able to watch the crowd. The men with the cooler were setting neatly vacuum-packed meat packages on the table tops while the women set up the tumbler and checked the roll of red raffle tickets. Stella was smiling and quietly singing along with the chorus. I motioned for her to join me on the small bandstand, but she shook her head and continued to lean against the wall behind the firemen.

When the song ended, Vern took the opportunity to get everyone's attention. "The women's auxiliary is now selling meat raffle tickets. It looks like we have an especially tasty assortment of beef, chicken, and pork. Tickets are five dollars each or five for twenty bucks. The winner gets his or her choice of whatever is on the table. The person with the number one less than the winner can have a free beer, wine, or mixed drink. The drawing will start at 8:00 sharp, and we'll draw another number after each song." He nodded to me. "Now, our entertainment will go on."

A few more people entered the bar as Vern made his announcement. Distracted by tuning my B string, I failed to notice the group of Whistling Pines residents who stepped in. Kathy Christensen surprised me by calling out, "How about some Kenny Rogers!"

After making eye contact with Kathy, I nodded, then saw Sherry Vogel seating the group at a long table with eight residents. "It appears that my duet partner has arrived!" I announced as I pulled a second bar stool aside for Sherry.

She blushed, then shook her head.

I waved for her to join me. "Come on, folks. Sherry Vogel has a wonderful voice, but she's a little shy about singing in public. Give her a hand."

Howard Johnson touched Sherry's shoulder and whispered something to her. She nodded, then walked toward me as the veterans applauded.

"What Kenny Rogers songs do you know?" I whispered to her.

Smiling at the crowd, Sherry whispered, "Who is Kenny Rogers?"

I was suddenly aware of our generation gap. "Are you old enough to be in a bar?"

"I'm twenty-one...if you round off my age."

I inwardly grimaced as I continued to smile for the crowd. "What classic country songs do you know?"

"Um, none come to mind."

"How about a recent country song?"

""Grease" by Lainey Wilson."

I strummed the opening, then nodded to Sherry, who sang, "It's been a long hot summer..."

Hardly anyone in the crowd recognized the lyrics, but they started tapping their toes to the lively song. We finished to polite applause as the Ladies Auxiliary moved through the crowd selling raffle tickets.

"What now?" Sherry asked.

""Boot Scootin' Boogie?""

Sherry's mouth opened, but nothing came out. A moment later, as she was typing into her phone, she whispered, "I've danced to that song. Stall while I look up the lyrics."

I played the long guitar intro, which got everyone's attention. Sherry's head was bobbing to the beat as she scanned through screens of the song's lyrics.

I began singing, "Out in the country past the city limit signs..."

Rocking along, Sherry smiled and waited to join me in the chorus, "Heel, toe, do-si-do..." Many of the patrons sang along, and three of the women who'd been seated with the Vietnam era vets got up and started to line dance.

I whispered to Sherry, "Do you know the second verse?"

She nodded and sang, "The bartender asked me, son, what'll it be..."

By the second chorus seven people were dancing, including Stella Hygge and one of the other firemen.

When the song ended some called out, "My Maria!"

Sherry shrugged, "I only know the chorus."

I started the song and continued until the chorus, where Ronnie Dunn sings the falsetto. Sherry sang, "My Maria..." while I sang the counter chorus, "Oh, Maria, I love you..."

Sherry seemed stunned when the crowd stood and clapped. I nudged her. "Take a bow."

Blushing, she nodded to the folks, then turned to me. "That was epic."

When the applause stopped, Vern stepped over to us and faced the crowd. Looking at his watch, he said, "Last chance to buy your raffle tickets. We'll draw the first number in five minutes."

I leaned my guitar against the wall and sat on a stool. "You did really well."

Sherry bit her lip and stared at the guitar. "I've never had *that* happen before."

"What's *that*?"

"It was like an out-of-body experience. I mean, I was singing, but it wasn't me. The people were clapping and dancing and..." She looked up and said, "It was magical."

Smiling, I replied, "Welcome to the world of performing."

"Does that happen to you every time you perform in front of people?"

"Not every time, but often. It's special. Savor that feeling."

Sherry looked toward the Whistling Pines group, drew a breath, and let it out. "I should get back to our people."

"Check on them, then come back for the next song."

"I don't know many more country songs these people would recognize."

"They'll be happy to hear whatever we perform." I paused, then added, "Except Taylor Swift. I doubt there are many Swifties in this audience."

One of the ticket sellers approached me. "Do you have five bucks, Doc?"

Pulling out my wallet, I handed her a twenty. "Who told you I was called Doc?"

Tearing off five tickets, the woman handed me half of each, putting the other half into a basket. "Vern told us about you. He also said you don't appreciate being recognized for your heroism."

"I'm not a hero," I replied, slipping the tickets into my wallet.

The woman smiled and put her hand on my wallet. "Keep those tickets handy. You might win a rump roast."

I put the tickets into my pocket, then returned my wallet to my back pocket as the ticket seller walked toward the bingo roller. Two more firemen walked in just in time to buy raffle tickets before the drawing.

Howard Johnson walked over and stood next to me, surveying the crowd. "This is the biggest crowd I've ever seen in the VFW. There are usually only a bunch of us old farts and our wives here for the meat raffle. The bachelor party and your music have really filled the place."

Virtually every seat was taken, with more firemen than seats at the rear tables. "It's as busy as the Christmas lutefisk feed," I observed.

Howard chuckled. "But less stinky." He patted my shoulder. "A few of the vets are grumbling about the firemen diluting their odds of winning the meat raffle."

"Is that a problem?"

"Only in their minds," Howard replied, patting my shoulder before turning to return to the Whistling Pines table.

"Howard..."

He turned back toward me.

"Is Alma Kotter cooking in that big mink coat?"

Looking toward the woman, Howard nodded and shrugged. "She wears it all the time. I think it's her *look*."

The bingo roller rumbled as the handle cranked. Ticket stubs rose and fell, while the room quieted in anticipation of a winner being announced. Dean Weske, the official tumbler operator, stopped cranking and opened the trap door. He reached in and drew out a ticket. "The winning number is..." He slowly read the ten-digit number. Letting the anticipation build, he then read the last two digits.

Everyone was staring at their tickets, some with their fingers following the numbers as Dean read them. After the last number was read, there was silence. Everyone looked around the room, waiting for the winner to shout and wave his ticket or to at least stand. Sparky and I seemed to be the only people not staring at their tickets. I felt a sinking feeling, remembering the unread tickets in my pocket. I pulled them out but couldn't remember the winning number. "What were the last numbers?"

"813," Dean said, reading from the winning stub.

In dread, I checked my numbers, remembering Jenny's concern about winning a tray of unrefrigerated meat. I sighed in relief, realizing I didn't have the winner.

Sparky stood, then nearly fell. Steadying himself on the nearest chair, he said, "I won!"

A collective groan came from the other side of the room, when they realized that a fireman would have the first pick of the displayed meat packages. As Sparky crossed the room, I took his arm as if steadying him, then whispered, "Choose the package of liver."

Sparky froze and stared at me as if he didn't understand. "I don't like liver."

"I don't care. Give it to your mother. Take the package of liver. Come on, I'll help you."

We walked together to the displayed meat, and I steered Sparky away from the steaks, chops, and roasts, toward the rusty brown lump of vacuum-packed calf liver. "Sparky's taking the liver!" I announced to the crowd.

A chuckle rippled through the regulars, relieved that the premium cuts were still up for the next drawing.

Muttering to me as we returned to the laughing firemen, Sparky said, "I don't even like liver."

As I seated Sparky among the firemen, I announced, "It's a bachelor party tradition for the groom to win the package of liver." That brought a round of laughter.

Vern announced the person holding ticket 812 was the winner of a free drink and still eligible for the meat drawing. One of the Vietnam vets jumped up and walked to the bar to collect his winning drink. I motioned for Sherry to return to the empty stool next to me.

As she sat, I whispered, ""Ghost Riders in the Sky.""

"I don't know that song," she whispered back.

"Sing the chorus. 'Yippee-I-oh, yippee-I-aye, ghost riders in the sky.'"

"Okay," she said, settling onto the stool.

In the commotion, I noticed the front door open and close without anyone entering. It seemed odd, but I was focused on starting the next song, until I heard the opening of "The Stripper" playing from a spot near the door. Anticipating the arrival of an exotic dancer, many in the crowd stood and turned toward the door. I rushed for the door, hoping to intercept the *entertainer* before she got inside, which diverted my attention from the Whistling Pines group, who were seated on the opposite side of the bar.

Blocking the door, I stared at the boombox that was blaring music, as people started hooting and whistling behind me. I turned just in time to see Alma Kotter strutting provocatively to the music, moving toward the fireman. Acutely aware of Alma's wish to repeat Ava Gardner's flashing of Frank Sinatra at every opportunity, I tried to push my way through the crowd before the great reveal. I waved at Sherry, who was near Alma, hoping she'd intervene before Alma shed her mink coat. As confused as much of the crowd was, Sherry sat in stunned silence as Alma strutted closer and closer to the firemen.

"No! Stop her!" I yelled, my voice drowned out by the blaring music and hooting crowd.

I was nearly past the Vietnam vets when Alma, facing away from me, pulled her mink open wide, exposing what I assumed was her bare 80-year-old wrinkled, sagging body to the firemen. I expected them to groan and turn their heads, but in their drunken state, they were all getting into Alma's performance.

Stella dashed forward and pulled Alma's mink coat closed, leading to boos and hisses from the crowd. Finally realizing what was happening, Sherry joined Stella. Together, they held the mink closed and escorted Alma back to her seat.

The door opened as I reached down to switch off the boombox, and Wendy stepped inside. Smiling like a Cheshire Cat, she asked, "Did I miss the entertainment?"

"You were the one who demanded there not be any strippers at the bachelor party."

"I don't think Alma's performance rises to the level of a bachelor party stripper."

"Geesh, Wendy. You could've warned me."

"That would've ruined the surprise."

Grabbing the boombox, Wendy disappeared out the door.

Vern met me halfway across the room, a smile across his usually stern face. "That was about the saddest striptease I've ever seen."

"I suppose the vision of Alma's naked body is burned into your retinas."

"Trust me, Peter, I've seen worse in my lifetime." He put his hand on my shoulder. "Play another song, and then Dean can draw another number."

After retrieving the guitar, I turned to Sherry. "That'll be a hard act to follow."

"Play something fun."

"Suggest something you know."

"Red Solo Cup."

I laughed, then played the short guitar intro before singing, "Red solo cup, I fill you up..."

As the laughter and clapping died down, Vern announced the next drawing. Dean Weske rolled the tickets and made a dramatic drawing from the tumbler as he did the first time, "And the winner is!"

He slowly read the numbers, knowing that everyone had the same first six numbers. Slowing as he got to the last digits, he read, "Eight." Then paused. "One." Several people groaned knowing they weren't winners. "Four!"

Again, the room went quiet with everyone awaiting the cheer from the person holding the winning ticket. Seeing the delay and knowing most people had purchased a string of tickets with consecutive numbers, I grimaced and looked at Sparky, who was now beyond reading his own ticket numbers. Stella stepped over and picked up Sparky's string of tickets. After reading the number, she sighed and announced, "The groom has won again."

A collective groan arose from the crowd as Stella helped Sparky stand, then stagger toward the meat display. Several women were staring daggers at Sparky as he swayed in front of the meat display. With Sparky apparently unable to make a choice, Stella reached out and grabbed a package. As she turned Sparky around for a trip back to the firemen, she announced, "Sparky has chosen a package of chicken wings!"

Sparky froze. "I don't like chicken wings."

Stella shoved him toward the firemen. "Shut up and go back with the other guys."

She tossed the package of wings to one of the women who seemed the most put out by Sparky's second win. "Courtesy of the Two Harbors Fire Department."

Sensing the rising hostility, Vern pointed at me. "Sing!"

I looked at Sherry, who shrugged. "Ghost Riders in the Sky."

I started playing the long guitar intro as people returned to their seats. "An old cowpoke was riding out one dark and windy day..."

Sherry joined in on the chorus as did most of the crowd. "Yipp-I-ay..."

As the applause died, several cell phones chimed loudly. The firemen simultaneously reached for the phones. Stella was the first to take a step toward the door. "Clear the way. We've got a fire."

Grabbing my shirt as she passed, Stella shouted, "Get Sparky to the fire. I'll drive and get the rest of these drunks on the truck."

Her words were delivered with such authority they almost made me salute and reply, "Yes, ma'am."

Chapter 15

Getting Sparky to my car was only the beginning of my problems. Buckling him into the seat, I asked, "Where's the fire?"

His eyes went wide. "What fire? There's a fire? We should get going."

"I would if I knew where it was," I replied, a little too testily.

"It's on the dispatcher's text."

"I'm not a fireman. I didn't receive a text."

"Do you want to join? We're always looking for new recruits."

I put my hand on Sparky's shoulder. "Look at your phone and give me the address you were sent."

Sparky patted his pockets and showed me his empty hands. "I don't know where my phone is."

"Listen, Sparky, I'm not going to dig through your pockets. Look again."

Sparky patted his front and back pants pockets. "Nope. Nothing."

"Is it on your belt?"

Sparky's look of revelation was almost comical. "Sure! That's where it is."

When he made no effort to reach for his phone, I said. "Can you reach it? Check the dispatcher's text for the fire's address."

"I can do that." He reached for his waist with his right hand, and I heard a metallic snapping sound, followed by a clunk. "Dang! I dropped it. I think it slid under the seat."

I heard the distant whine of a siren as I tipped my head back in frustration. "Try to get it."

He leaned to the right but gave up immediately. "My hand's too fat."

After unbuckling my seatbelt, I jogged to the passenger's side and opened the door. The space between the seat and the threshold was indeed narrow. I wiggled my fingers into the space but could barely touch something smooth with my fingertips. Reaching under the seat, I released the latch, which caused the seat to jerk back, surprising Sparky.

"Easy, Doc. I'm susceptible to motion sickness."

"Shut up while I look under your seat."

Struggling to get my shoulders past Sparky's knees, I gave him a gentle push. He responded by leaning away from me and farting.

"Jeez, Sparky. Hold the next one until my face is away from your butt."

He responded by sliding toward the driver's seat and pulling his legs up. "Is that better?"

Still unable to do more than touch Sparky's phone, I opened the back door, got on my knees, and probed under the seat with my fingers. I touched the flat surface of the phone but couldn't coax it toward me. Adjusting my position, I pushed my hand farther under the seat and put my fingers onto the phone. It started to slide toward me when the car rolled ahead.

"What the hell are you doing, Sparky?"

"Is this little handle the parking brake?"

"Pull it up and leave your hands off everything else!"

I had to readjust my position to reach under the seat again. Touching the phone, I tried to slide it back with my fingertips.

"Doc, why does your car have three pedals? What's this extra one for?"

"Keep your feet off the pedals!"

The engine revved as I slid the phone free. "This long one must be the gas, like in my pickup truck. Why do you have two brake pedals?"

"It's a stick shift," I replied, as I uncoiled myself from under the backseat.

"Stick shifts have two brakes?"

"The left pedal is the clutch." No sooner were the words out of my mouth than I heard the grinding of gears.

"That's right. You push that so you can shift."

I was still on my knees when the car lurched forward, banging my ribs on the doorframe, and knocking me to the floor. Luckily, Sparky wasn't adept at easing the clutch out, so his quick clutching caused the engine to stall.

The episode caused a massive release of adrenaline. I reacted quickly, jumping up, slamming the back door, racing to the driver's door, and pulling Sparky out of the seat. I handed him the phone. "Get in on the passenger side and check your texts for the fire address."

A second siren whined as I took my seat. Pulling the door closed with my left hand caused a shot of pain reminiscent of when the bull moose butted me.

"Here's the address, Doc. It's just a few blocks from the lighthouse."

Clamping my arm hard against my ribs made the pain almost tolerable, I restarted the car, shifted it into gear, released the parking brake, and eased out of the parking spot.

Sparky frowned at me. "Doc, we're going to a fire. Could you drive a little faster?"

Not screaming in frustration took all the control I could muster. "We're going there now, Sparky. If you hadn't dropped your damn phone under the seat, we'd already be there."

"If you hadn't played under the seat for five minutes, we'd have...left five minutes ago!"

I turned at the first corner and accelerated, causing Sparky to grab the door rest and parking brake handle. "Easy, Doc. I think I'm going to be sick."

"Choke it back until we get to the fire," I said, having no reserve of sympathy.

"Stop the car, Doc. I'm going to chuck my cookies."

Braking hard, I pulled to the curb as Sparky threw his door open. I looked away, listening to his retching.

After a couple of minutes, he sat up and pulled the door closed. "Okay. I think I had a bad beer at the bar."

"We were at the VFW."

"That explains it. Those vets don't like to hang around with us civilians." Having said that, Sparky turned toward me with a look of near fear. "My guts don't like that brand of beer."

"What brand is that?" I asked, trying to determine the exact location of the distant flashing red lights.

"The brown kind with bubbles."

"Sparky, all beer is brown with bubbles."

"I think I'm allergic to something in it. Maybe it's the yeast." His eyes went wide, and I braked hard and turned to the curb as he let loose with the mother of all burps.

"Why did you stop? We're on our way to a fire!"

I pulled away from the curb and turned down a street toward several sets of flashing red lights. As we approached the fire trucks, Sparky let loose with another fart.

"My god, Sparky. You've got gas coming from both ends."

"Like I said, the yeast and I don't get along. It's almost as bad as when I eat cabbage rolls."

I stopped behind Kerry's unmarked police car. Sparky ran toward the firemen who were directing a stream of water into a burning garage. Kerry looked at me, his face lit by flames shooting out of the building and the strobe effect of flashing red and blue lights.

"What took you so long?" Kerry asked without looking away from the fire.

"Sparky dropped his phone under the car seat."

"And it took you five minutes to find it?"

I drew a breath, doubling me over with a jolt of pain into my ribs.

"What did you do to yourself this time, sailor?"

"I think I broke a rib when Sparky released the parking brake. Either that, or it was when he popped the clutch."

"Why did you let Sparky drive? Isn't he drunk?"

"He wasn't driving. I moved him to the driver's seat after he farted in my face."

Without looking away from the fire, Kerry chuckled. "Are you Abbott or Costello in that comedy act?"

Still doubled over, I groaned. "Call Jenny. I need a ride to the hospital."

"It's that bad, huh?"

"Yeah," I croaked.

Kerry walked to the passenger door of his unmarked car. "Let's not disturb Jenny until we know how bad it is. Get in."

Contacting dispatch, Kerry told them he was arriving with an injury from the fire scene. I frowned at him. "They're going to think there's a burn victim or an injured fireman on the way."

"Maybe."

"Don't you think that's overstating the emergency?"

"Nah," Kerry replied as he turned on his siren and flashers. "The on-call doctor is probably napping. This way he'll be awake when we arrive."

As Kerry predicted, we were met at the emergency entrance by a crew of three people who had a gurney ready for whatever injury appeared. A young man pulled open my door and knelt beside me. "What's going on?"

"I may have broken ribs."

"What makes you think that?"

Kerry joined the young man at my side. "The patient is a Navy corpsman. He's dealt with a lot of things. If he thinks he's got broken ribs, I'd bet that he does."

A woman in scrubs joined the young man. "Can you get out of the car by yourself?" she asked.

"I hope so. If you have to help me, it's going to hurt like hell."

"What's your name, sailor?"

"Peter Rogers."

"His friends call him, Doc."

"Well, Doc Rogers, I'm Sheila Larson, the on-call doctor. How bad is your break? Are you coughing blood or wheezing?"

The male orderly helped me swing my legs out of the car, then he stepped back to see if I could stand without assistance. "I doubt that I have a pneumothorax. I'm not coughing up blood, so we're probably just dealing with the pain from the break."

I caught Dr. Larson's glance at Kerry and her smirk. "He knows the right words," she whispered to Kerry.

"Yeah, but he's not too smart. How did you break your ribs last time, Doc?"

"A moose butted me," I said as I slowly stood.

"Wasn't there something important you had to do the next day?"

Glaring at Kerry, I took a small step toward the gurney. "I got married the next day."

Dr. Larson tried to hide her laugh, unsuccessfully. "I bet you were a ball of fun on the honeymoon."

"Yeah," I said as I was eased onto the gurney. "My wife had a lovely time sitting in our private suite's hot tub."

"Honeymoons are overrated," Kerry said as I laid back. "They're a vacation, but let's be serious, you'd consummated your relationship long before the wedding."

The doctor laughed. "Oh no! I've never heard of that happening before." She turned to the nurse. "How about you, Josie?"

Josie, who had gray hair peeking out from under her scrub cap, smiled. "It might've happened once or twice. These darned Norwegian Lutherans breed like rabbits."

"Hey!" Larson protested. "We're just loving people."

Kerry kept his hand on the edge of the gurney as I was rolled inside. "Are you Swedish or Norwegian, Doc?"

"It doesn't matter."

"You're probably right. Sweden and Norway were one country until when, 1914? It's all one big gene pool."

"It was 1905," I corrected.

"Take him to X-ray Josie. Let's see how badly those ribs are broken."

Chapter 16

The Toradol in my IV was slowly kicking in. Its effect was mostly anti-inflammatory, but the pain was muted, if not hidden. Dr. Larson's grin was slightly concerning when she entered the room. "It appears you'll live," she said.

"Turn me loose," I replied.

"How do you plan to get home..." she glanced at the large clock mounted on the wall over the computer, "...at 3:20 AM?"

"I'll call an Uber."

Larson snorted. "Did you just move here? An Uber? Really?" She paused, assessing my state of mind. "Your wife is listed as your emergency contact. Do you want to call her, or should I ask the nurse to make the call?"

"We have two kids who are sound asleep. I'll walk."

Larson put her hands on her hips and gave me a stern look, conveying her displeasure. "I thought you were a combat medic."

I corrected her, "Navy corpsman."

"Whatever. You know as well as I do that the Toradol is a Band-Aid that'll mask some of your pain. It's not intended to allow you to do something stupid like trying to walk several miles. My discharge orders will specify that you not lift anything, climb stairs, operate any motor vehicles, or walk any farther than to the bathroom for ten days. That'll allow your broken ribs time to heal enough to withstand a fall without puncturing a lung."

"Our bedroom is on the second floor."

"No stairs means you won't be sleeping in your bedroom. Understood?"

"Yes, ma'am."

Larson's look softened, and she approached the side of my hospital bed. "Let me give you something for the pain."

"No, ma'am. Narcotics have all kinds of side effects, are addictive, and cause other problems. The Toradol is all I need."

"I can't tell you how much I hate dealing with you macho types. The pain can cause shock, which you know can kill."

"The pain is God's way of making sure I don't do any of those stupid things you mentioned."

"You could use a couple milligrams of Diazepam. It would take the edge off your stubborn attitude."

"Don't suggest that to my wife. She might agree with you."

The sound of footsteps in the hallway preceded the entrance of Deb Stone. The doctor turned and asked, "Are you married to this mule-headed sailor?"

Deb smiled at the description. "Tonight, I'm his chauffeur." She looked past the doctor. "Are you ready to go home?"

"Did Jenny send you?"

Deb shook her head. "Kerry said you were here and in need of a ride. I thought I'd let Jenny and the kids sleep."

"What about your sleep?"

"Being married to the police chief means having my sleep interrupted a couple of nights a week by phone calls. I've become accustomed to napping when I can."

Dr. Larson turned and said, "I'll print out my discharge instructions." She stopped next to Deb and added, "Tell his wife to strap him to the couch and give him a bottle to pee in for the next week."

Deb walked to the bedside and took my hand. "Kerry said your life is an ongoing dumpster fire."

"Why didn't Kerry collect me?"

"He's still at the fire scene. There's some question about the origin, so he's guarding it until an arson inspector arrives." Deb paused. "How bad is the pain?"

"On a scale of one to ten, I'd put it at eight."

"You damn sailors and soldiers think you're so tough. I suppose a ten would be when you've been shot and are bleeding out on the floor."

"Yup, that'd be a ten. My pain is only an eight."

"Can you take a deep breath?"

I started to inhale but quickly stopped. "Nope."

"Sparky is getting married tomorrow, and you're supposed to be his best man."

I looked past Deb at the door to make sure the doctor wasn't standing there. "Keep your voice down."

"Oh, no. You're *not* planning to attend the wedding."

"Yes, I *am* attending the wedding."

"The doctor just said Jenny should strap you to the couch and give you a urinal."

"I think she said a bottle to pee in, not a urinal."

"Damn it, Rogers! Falling down could kill you."

"I don't plan to fall."

A nurse swept into the room carrying a sheaf of papers. "Dr. Larson said she's explained the restrictions to you. Correct?"

Before I could reply, Deb said, "He heard them. He just doesn't plan to follow them."

The nurse shook her head. "Welcome to my world." She handed the papers to me along with a pen. "Sign the top sheet at the bottom. It acknowledges your understanding of the instructions...even if you don't plan to follow them."

As soon as the nurse walked out of the room, I handed everything to Deb. As I sat on the edge of the bed, she accepted the instructions. "Give me a minute to get out of this hospital gown and into my clothes."

Deb stepped back and watched me grimace when I reached for the bag containing my belongings. "Are you sure you don't need a hand?"

"I love you dearly, Deb. But you're not helping me put on underwear."

"Listen, tough guy. You've got nothing I haven't already seen."

"You may have seen men's plumbing before, but you've never seen *my* plumbing. Turn your back."

Struggling to get my legs into my underwear left me exhausted. "Okay. I could use a hand with the pants and shirt."

Deb turned and looked at me. My torso was wrapped in an Ace bandage, and the rest of my body covered with a sheen of sweat after the exertion of pulling on underwear. "And you think you're going to a wedding tomorrow?"

I slipped my arms into my shirt as Deb held them out for me. "I *AM* going to a wedding tomorrow. End of discussion."

"Jenny may have something to say about that."

"I'm sure she will," I replied.

The nurse walked back in and handed a small white bag to Deb. "The pharmacy filled an order for Percocet, just in case *Mr. Tough Guy* decides to yield the moral high ground."

* * *

Jenny walked downstairs when she heard our voices in the kitchen. Not fully awake, she frowned when she saw Deb Stone. "You went to the bachelor party, Deb?"

Chuckling, Deb replied, "No, I retrieved your injured husband from the emergency room."

Jenny pulled her robe tight around herself as she processed that information. "The emergency room? What happened at the bachelor party?"

I grabbed the back of a chair to support myself while Deb's conversation continued, "There was a fire call. Peter was driving Sparky to the fire and there was an incident."

"An accident? Is Sparky okay?"

With the pain becoming unbearable, I hobbled toward the living room. "It wasn't an accident."

"Apparently, something happened when Peter was retrieving Sparky's cell phone from under the car seat."

Jenny took my arm and helped me walk to the recliner, closest upholstered chair. I fell, as much as sat down, gasping in pain after the impact of my butt on the cushion.

"I'm going home to get a couple of hours of sleep," Deb announced. "Here are the hospital discharge papers and a bottle of Percocet. The doctor said you should strap him to the couch and give him a pee bottle."

Jenny squatted next to the chair, so we were eye to eye. "You're in a lot of pain. How are you going to deal with it?"

"I'd like a couple of Tylenol."

"Most sane people would take a Percocet."

"I guess I'm not that smart."

After squirming around to find the least uncomfortable position, I took a half breath and let it out. "Okay. I surrender. Give me half a Percocet and some crackers."

"How about a whole Percocet," Jenny said as she stood. "Let's get hold of the pain and knock it down. We'll talk about half Percocets and Tylenol after you can take a full breath. Okay?"

"Fine. But I'll only take them for a day."

Jenny walked to the kitchen and said, "This is our honeymoon all over again, isn't it?"

"Not at all. It's Sparky and Wendy's wedding. And there won't be any motel room with a hot tub overlooking Lake Superior."

"You're right. The hot tub overlooking the lake just wouldn't be the same with two kids in the room, would it?" I heard water running, followed by a cupboard door opening and closing. "On the other hand, you don't know how great that hot tub felt after being tense all of our wedding day. You were in bed, doped up on Percocet and unable to perform your wedding night duties."

"Could you speed up the delivery of the pain pill. I'm starting to hear the ghost of weddings past."

Kneeling next to the chair, Jenny handed me a stack of crackers and a glass of milk. "What were you thinking?"

"I was trying to reach for Sparky's phone under the seat. I didn't expect him to try driving away while I was hanging out of the back door."

Jenny handed me the white pill. "You're kidding?"

"Nope. He was drunk and had moved to the driver's seat to get out of my way. The next thing I knew, the car lurched ahead and I was in pain."

"Where's your car?"

"The last I saw, it was parked behind Kerry's squad car at the fire."

"Back up. What fire?"

"After the striptease…"

"There wasn't going to be a stripper! Where did you find a stripper?"

"Wendy put Alma Kotter up to it. Alma did her Ava Garner imitation while "The Stripper" played on a boombox."

"Alma stripped for the bachelor party? She's like eighty years old!"

"I know," I said as the warm sensation of pain relief swept over me. "Vern said she looks good for her age."

"Where were you?"

"Thankfully, I was behind her and didn't have a view of her…whatever."

“But Vern saw her naked.”

“Yeah, Vern and the firemen got an eyeful.”

Jenny giggled. “OMG. I suppose that’ll be the talk of Whistling Pines this week. Alma will be bragging about being the entertainment for a bachelor party.”

I slipped off to sleep.

Chapter 17

The Percocet wore off about the same time as Jeremy raced down the stairs, sounding like a buffalo stampede. Jenny was a step behind, shushing him while telling him to let me sleep.

"But *Mom*, it's Saturday morning. I want to watch TV."

"I'm awake," I croaked. "Life can go on."

After serving the kids breakfast, Jenny brought me a cup of coffee and a slice of toast. "I suggest you take another Percocet to keep the pain from getting out of control."

"I'm sure a couple of Tylenol will keep the edge off my pain."

"Peter, a couple of Tylenol will *not* keep the edge off the pain caused by broken ribs. That's especially true if you plan to do anything other than lay in the chair all day while taking shallow breaths."

Lifting the coffee mug to my lips caused a jolt of pain, making me slop hot coffee on my lap. Jenny's RN degree made her completely aware of how much pain I might be feeling and how the slopped coffee and resulting grimace, were signs of my reaction to the pain. Realizing the situation, I relented and said, "Fine. I'll take one Percocet to take the edge off. I'll switch to Tylenol at noon."

Jenny returned with a white tablet and a glass of water. "Make sure you take this with a bite of toast."

A brief knock on the door preceded Wendy's entrance. "Sparky's as sick as a dog and we're getting married in seven hours. What hangover remedy do you suggest?"

Jenny looked into the kitchen as Wendy stalked through. "He's probably dehydrated. Make sure he drinks lots of water."

"It's hard to drink water when you're hurling..." To her credit, Wendy realized Jeremy was listening intently to her. She composed her thoughts and continued, "when your tummy is already upset and you're not keeping things down."

"Don't push him to drink any volume of liquids. Start with a sip every five minutes. When he tolerates that, move him to swallows of Gatorade or orange juice."

Wendy frowned. "That will take forever. Don't you have a quick remedy? You know, like the hair of the dog?"

"The hair of the dog is *not* the best approach right now. Just try the water and graduate to Gatorade."

Wendy stopped at the door. "What's wrong with you, Peter? Why is there an Ace bandage wrapped around your chest?"

"Sparky and I had a little accident. I cracked a couple of ribs."

"Sparky didn't say anything about you getting hurt last night."

"Yeah. He might not remember that part of the evening."

"Will that bandage fit under your tuxedo?"

I tried to smile. "I'm sure it will."

Jenny cleared her throat. "Peter is taking pain pills. I'm not sure he'll be up to standing at the altar through a wedding ceremony. Do you have someone who could fill in?"

Wendy was stunned. "There's no one who will fit into Peter's tux. I mean, anyone else would have to wear a suit or..." some vision raced through her mind. "Or, one of the firemen would have to wear his dress uniform."

"The Two Harbors volunteer firemen have dress uniforms?" I asked.

"Don't they?" Wendy asked.

"I've never seen them wear anything dressier than matching blue shirts with their little badges pinned to them. I think most of them wear jeans with their uniform shirts."

"That would be unacceptable," Wendy announced. "Take whatever pills you need to get you through the ceremony."

Jenny stared at the kitchen door as Wendy stormed out. "Wendy's not very sympathetic."

"Sympathy isn't one of her superpowers," I replied.

Jeremy waited for us to stop talking before asking, "If Sparky is sick, are they still getting married?"

Jenny collected his cereal bowl and said, "I'm sure Sparky will be better by this afternoon."

"Will Dad be better, too?"

Jenny looked at me. "It's hard to say what's going to happen to your father. Broken ribs take weeks to heal."

Those words were barely out of Jenny's mouth when there was another knock at the back door. She looked at me and asked, "What's your bet, Wendy or Sparky?"

"None of the above," I replied.

Kerry and Deb Stone walked in, Deb carrying a crockpot, and Kerry with a bakery bag in his good hand. "We come bearing food!" Deb announced as she walked past Jenny to the kitchen counter. She plugged the crockpot in as Kerry set the white bag on the kitchen table.

"Why did you bring us a hotdish?" Jenny asked.

"Isn't that the traditional Lutheran gift delivered when someone is sick or injured?" Deb asked, craning her neck to look past Jenny so she could see me.

"Peter's not *that* sick," Jenny replied as she drifted toward the table to check out the bakery bag.

Kerry walked to the cupboard and took down mugs that he filled with coffee from the carafe. He carried the pot to the living room and topped off the mug sitting next to me, then whispered. "How sore are your ribs?"

"I just took a Percocet, so they're not too bad."

He nodded and asked, "Are you still planning to be Sparky's best man?"

"Yeah, for now."

Jenny, Deb, and Jeremy were moving pastries from the bag to a plate. Amy, who was intrigued by everyone's interest in the bag, tried to climb onto a chair. Jeremy boosted her up so she could lean on the table. Amy immediately reached for a doughnut covered with powdered sugar. Before any of the adults noticed, she'd taken a bite, covering her hands, face, shirt, and the table with white powder.

I watched from my chair, not inclined to test the pain-killing power of the Percocet by shouting out a warning.

"Would you like a Danish or doughnut?" Kerry asked.

"No, thanks. I'm not hungry."

Ignoring my comment, Deb ripped off a sheet of paper towel and carried a cherry-filled Danish pastry to me. "You need to keep up your strength." She set the pastry on my lap and smiled. "Hunger has nothing to do with eating a flaky Danish."

Lifting the pastry to my mouth caused only minor pain. As Deb suggested, the pastry was wonderful, although I really wasn't pleased by the trail of flakes deposited on my chest when I bit into it.

Jenny lifted the crockpot lid and inhaled. "You made us chili."

I noticed Kerry's grimace. "It's Scandinavian chili. You know, the kind without any seasoning. It's more of a hamburger, kidney bean, and tomato soup."

"Cut it out," Deb replied. "I seasoned it the same way my mother does, with brown sugar."

I must've groaned because the adults all looked at me as if I was taking my last breath.

"Sorry, did I say that out loud?"

Waving off their concern, Jenny said, "Ignore him. Percocet has removed his mental filter. He'll happily eat a bowlful later." She glared at me, then added, "Won't you, dear?"

Enough of my brain was still working to hesitate before making an inappropriate comment summarizing my true feelings about chili seasoned with brown sugar. Instead, I replied, "Yup."

With a coffee mug in one hand and a glazed doughnut in the other, Kerry sat near me on the sofa while Deb and Jenny cleaned up after Amy. "Dr. Robertson and I had a discussion," he whispered.

"Did he admit to breaking into my office?"

Kerry shook his head. "No, but he's very interested in the Army footlocker we dug up. He told me it's rightfully his as Astrid's heir."

"What did he say when you told him about your plan to involve the Korean embassy?"

Kerry paused while taking a bite of doughnut and making sure the women weren't listening. "He wasn't pleased by that plan."

"I assume he denied having any knowledge of the bloody dagger."

"He claimed to be unaware of the footlocker's exact contents, so knew nothing about the blood on the knife."

"What's happening with the silk wrapper and dagger? Is someone testing the blood?"

"The BCA has them. Their preliminary analysis confirmed that the blood is human, but that's as far as they've gotten."

"Have the librarians found any murder victims in the post-Korean war era?"

Kerry nodded slightly. "Maybe. A Two Harbors fisherman disappeared in 1953."

"What makes you think it might be connected to the knife in the footlocker?"

"There wasn't anything suspicious at the time. Commercial fishermen disappeared pretty regularly on Lake Superior, but Olaf Erickson owned the Gal Norske Fishing Company."

I tried to sit up in the recliner but was hit with a stabbing pain. "That can't be a coincidence."

Kerry unfolded a sheet of paper taken from his pocket. It was a copy made from the front page of the *Two Harbors Times*. "At the time, the sheriff declared Erickson's failure to return from his daily fishing trip a boating accident. However, Olaf and his boat disappeared when the lake was calm, and he never radioed in an SOS."

"My bet is that Eugene Tostenrud stabbed him, then sank the boat with Olaf onboard."

Kerry shrugged. "The boat was never located. We'll never know."

"What motive did Eugene have?"

"Love, money, alcohol, or drugs are the typical murder motives."

"Which would fit here?" I asked.

"That's a good question for your old folks."

"Or the dentist. He was probably a kid back then. He might've remembered his uncle having a dispute with the fisherman."

Kerry stood and smiled. "It'll be a topic for you to pursue when you're healed."

"Wait! Why me? It's a crime."

"Everyone involved is dead. It's an academic exercise, not a criminal investigation. Turn your librarians and the Whistling Pines residents loose on it."

Our conversation was interrupted by urgent pounding on the back door. Kerry took a step toward the kitchen, ready to act, as Jenny rushed to answer the door. Sparky, looking pale and wearing a t-shirt splattered with vomit gasped, "Come quick! We've got an emergency!"

Kerry, accustomed to dealing with frantic emergencies, stepped behind Jenny and asked, "What kind of an emergency?" He pulled out his phone and prepared to dial 911.

Surprised by Kerry's arrival at the door, Sparky stuttered, "Um, it's a female kind of emergency." He looked at Jenny, "Come quick. It's Wendy."

"Do you need an ambulance?" Kerry asked.

"Um, no. It's her dress."

Deb pushed Kerry aside and followed Jenny out of the door. Feeling an unrealistic need to assist, I struggled out of the recliner and then shuffled across the kitchen before feeling sweaty and fatigued.

"Jeremy, keep Amy out of trouble until I get back," I said as Kerry took my arm and helped me down the steps.

"You're not thinking too clearly, are you?" Kerry asked.

"Why would you say that?"

"You just left a middle-school kid in charge of his toddler sister."

"They'll be fine. We'll be back in a minute. What can go wrong?"

It took nearly two minutes for me to shuffle across the lawn to Sparky and Wendy's rental house. I heard Wendy wailing before we reached the property line. Deb and Jenny's voices were more subdued, but they conveyed urgency.

Inside, we stopped behind Sparky, who was standing in the bedroom doorway.

"Can't you unstick the zipper?" Wendy whined.

"It's not just stuck," Jenny explained.

"When was your last fitting?" Deb asked.

"Last week. Why?"

"Have you put on any weight since then?" Jenny asked.

"I've put on three pounds since then. Is that a problem?"

"Let's call your seamstress. Maybe she can do something," Jenny suggested.

"Nooo! She's working in Beaver Bay, running the Cove Point Lodge children's program. She can't get away."

"Safety pins!" Deb said. "We need a bunch of safety pins!"

Sparky spun around and bumped into Kerry, who bumped into me, causing a jolt of pain. Grabbing Kerry's lapel, Sparky said, "Get me to the safety pin store! Red lights and siren!"

Deb edged past Sparky and spoke to Kerry. "We need safety pins to close the gap in Wendy's zipper."

"I've never bought a safety pin. Who carries them?"

"The hardware store! Go!"

Sparky tried to push past Kerry and me in the narrow hallway, causing a jam of bodies. Kerry grabbed Sparky's shoulders. "Get into your tux. I'll get the safety pins."

"Oh, geez, yah. Good idea."

Kerry guided me out of the door and onto the lawn. "I can do this faster without you. Go home and keep an eye on your kids."

"I need to put my tux on, too," I said.

"Really?" he asked as he rushed to his car. "Do you think you're going to be in a wedding this afternoon?"

Kerry's tires squealed as he pulled away from the curb. I shuffled back to our house to check on my children. The aroma of the sweet chili hit my nose as soon as I opened the door. The lid was off the crockpot and a ladle was laying on the counter, dripping chili. I followed the trail of slopped chili from the kitchen to the dining room. Jeremy was eating chili. He'd somehow wrangled Amy into the highchair and put a bowl of chili on her tray. While that was a fine plan, the reality was that Amy was having fun banging a spoon against the bowl and flinging kidney beans and bits of meat into the air.

Wanting to scream, but feeling unnaturally calm, probably because of the painkillers, I smiled and watched them. Jeremy had done pretty much as I'd asked. And Amy was being a toddler without close adult supervision. Rather than dealing with any of the chaos, I ladled a bowl of chili for myself and sat down across from Jeremy.

"I like Mrs. Stone's chili. It's sweeter than yours."

"She uses a different recipe," I replied as a kidney bean flew past my face and stuck to the wall.

Jeremy looked at me, then at the kidney bean slid down the wall, leaving a streak of tomato sauce. "Aren't you going to yell and clean that up?"

"Nope."

Jeremy frowned. "This is really weird, Dad. You're acting like a kid."

"Yup."

"Aren't you going to take away Amy's bowl?"

"Nope."

"She might break it."

I ate another spoonful of chili and said, "Maybe."

Looking disgusted, Jeremy got up and carried his bowl and spoon to the kitchen. A minute later, he was back with a damp sponge and paper towels. Removing Amy's bowl, he wiped her face and shirt with paper towels before using the sponge on her face, then the highchair tray. Checking to see if I was jumping in, but seeing me only eating and not parenting, he picked the kidney bean off the wall as he went past. "I expect more allowance if you're going to make me behave like an adult," he said from the kitchen.

I was putting my bowl into the sink when I heard Kerry's car brake to a stop. Jeremy and Amy were in the living room playing with big plastic blocks. I struggled up the stairs, found the tux I'd rented for the wedding, and struggled again to put it on.

Jenny rushed into the bedroom and froze, seeing me in the tux. "You're planning to go to the wedding? Really?"

"I think I'm giving away the bride...or something."

Jenny stripped off her jeans and sweatshirt, then changed into her bridesmaid's dress.

"Did you get Wendy pinned in?" I asked as she hurried around putting on makeup and brushing her hair.

"As long as she doesn't try to do the "Hokey-Pokey" she'll probably be okay. But any quick moves might result in a major wardrobe malfunction."

"Major as in, a seam will tear out?"

Jenny stopped and looked at me. "Major as in people will see way more tattoos than anyone knows that Wendy has."

Intrigued, I said, "Give me an example."

"She's got a leprechaun and a rainbow on her abdomen."

"What's so shocking about that?"

"There's a pot of gold at the end of the rainbow."

In my drug-induced stupor, I tried to reason through the thought and how it might be arranged on Wendy's anatomy.

Jenny looked up as she put on her second shoe. Seeing my frown, she said, "You just figured it out, didn't you?"

"I think so."

"Let me tell you, it's not a vision I'll soon banish from my memory."

Jenny straightened her dress and looked in the mirror. "I look okay, right?"

"You look great." I had a sudden thought. "Wait! What about the kids?"

"Deb and Kerry are watching them."

We waved at Deb, Kerry, and the kids as Jenny ushered me through the dining room. Jenny gave Deb a hug and we walked out. I took out my car keys, but Jenny snatched them from my hand. "You're on drugs. You are *not* driving."

The car ride made me mildly nauseous, and I was happy when Jenny parked at the Moose Lodge, the wedding venue. While not enormous, it was as large as most of the churches in town and was willing to host a non-denominational wedding service. The chairs were already filling when we arrived and I noticed Wendy's band, The Gin Fizzes, setting up their instruments behind the lectern that was doubling as the celebrant's podium for the ceremony.

Before I could greet anyone, a photographer guided me to the front of the hall where I stood next to Sparky for a couple of pictures. Wendy and Jenny arrived a moment later and a few more pictures were taken, then the photographer moved us in front of the gathering.

I recognized Sparky's mother, standing alone in the front row looking like she'd sucked a lemon. Next to her were other guests in suits and dresses, who I assumed were Sparky's relatives. Behind them were firemen, all wearing their dark blue shirts and jeans with their tiny silver badges pinned on their shirts. I saw Stella Hygge staring at me. She gestured, squeezing her ribs. I nodded, indicating that my ribs were okay.

On the bride's side of the aisle were the staff from Whistling Pines, who we referred to as our work family. Sherry Vogel waved to me, looking far different from her usual t-shirt and jeans. She wore a modest red sheath dress.

A noise behind me caught my attention and I turned to find Brian Johnson standing behind the lectern in a dark suit that looked remarkably like a band uniform. "You're performing the ceremony?" I asked.

"I've been ordained by the Brotherhood of the Order of Orchestral Brass."

One of the firemen in the crowd said, "Brian is one of the BOOBs," which brought a round of laughter from the gathered group.

"What seminary did you attend?" I asked.

"The Correspondence School of Pawtucket."

"Pawtucket?"

"Pawtucket is the home of the Brotherhood."

"Was it a long course of study?" Jenny asked.

Brian chuckled. "It took me about five minutes to fill out the online application. My email ordination certificate arrived within minutes. Do you want to see the copy I printed?"

Before I could reply, Brian pulled a sheet of paper from his suit coat pocket, displaying his certificate, which looked suitable for framing. I examined the certificate more closely. "It is issued to *Brain* Johnson, not *Brian* Johnson."

Waving off my concern, he returned the certificate to his pocket. "Let's consider it a use of my symbolic title, rather than it being a typo."

"Isn't that going to cause a problem with the marriage license?"

Brian considered that question. "I'll just sign it as 'Brain Johnson' so the two documents match."

Confused, but unable to offer a solution, I asked, "Which version of the Bible does the brotherhood use? Revised Standard or King James?"

"The BOOBs leave that choice up to the individual clergy," he replied. "I prefer the NIRV edition of the Bible."

"NIRV?" I asked.

"The New International Revised Version. It's written at a third-grade level. Some of the parables are translated as humorous anecdotes."

"Of course, you'd prefer that translation."

"Do you want to hear the story about 'John the speedy Disciple?'"

"Not really."

Undeterred, Brian explained how John outran Peter to Jesus' burial tomb. "The book of John explains how he was the speedy apostle. Of course, Peter is known as the better swimmer."

Before he could explain Peter's swimming prowess, Brian was interrupted when the Gin Fizzes' bass player started playing a riff that silenced the crowd. A moment later, the guitar and organ joined him, playing the Disney version of "Lady and the Tramp." Howard Johnson escorted Wendy down the aisle between the folding chairs. Hulda Packer followed, pushing her walker and throwing rose petals from a basket attached to the front frame.

With Wendy and Sparky facing each other, Brian made introductory remarks about the sanctity of marriage. Wendy squirmed about halfway through the remarks. I heard a safety pin hit the floor. Jenny, who held the wedding bouquet, glanced down and spotted the silver safety pin at Wendy's feet. She looked at me with fear in her eyes.

Brian, never one to miss a chance to revel in the limelight, dragged out his introduction. Wendy momentarily let go of Sparky's left hand and pulled up the bodice of her strapless dress, causing another safety pin to let loose and fly toward the crowd.

With everyone else focused on Brian's comments, Wendy looked frantic. Realizing that I was the only other person who'd seen the safety pin fly, she looked at me and mouthed, "Uh oh."

Oblivious to the impending wardrobe malfunction, Brian was dutifully working his way through the correspondence school wedding manual. He asked Sparky to read his vows. While Sparky fumbled with a stack of recipe cards featuring what was probably a heartfelt expression of his undying love, I leaned forward and whispered, "Cut to the chase. Your bride's dress is about to blow."

To his credit, Sparky paused and assessed the increasing problem Wendy was having keeping her boobs covered by the slowly descending dress. Stuffing the cards into his pocket, he said, "I do."

Taken by surprise by the quick move to the end of the ceremony, Brian turned to Wendy and said, "You may now read your vows."

Grasping the top of her dress firmly with her right hand to stop additional southward movement, Wendy simply said, "I do."

Brian scanned the directions manual to find the next item in the wedding ceremony. "The band will now play a song apparently made famous by the group, Confederate Railroad."

As the band played the opening of "Trashy Women," I glanced at the crowd. The more traditional attendees, wearing suits and dresses, seemed shocked. The less traditional, in firemen's uniforms and jeans, seemed to be rocking. For the most part, the

Whistling Pines residents knew Wendy well enough to expect the unexpected from her wedding music.

When the song ended, Brian did the ring exchange, then said, "If there is anyone here who knows why these two..."

I saw Sparky's mom, her face approaching the color of a ripe plum, preparing to stand and respond to the offer to, "speak now or forever hold your peace."

Stepping behind Brian, I held out my arms as if imploring the blessing of a higher being, I said, "By virtue of his correspondence school diploma from the Brotherhood Order of Orchestral Brass, Brian pronounces Sparky and Wendy, husband and wife."

Brian glanced over his shoulder at me, then rolled with the situation and said, "You may kiss the bride."

Sparky reached out and embraced Wendy, planting a lingering kiss. As he squeezed her, safety pins started flying to the floor, and the top of Wendy's wedding gown slipped to precarious levels.

Jenny, always thinking on her feet, said, "Group hug!"

Pushing Brian toward the couple, I moved between the crowd and the wedding party, throwing my arms over both Wendy and Sparky's shoulders as the band started a Jimi Hendrix-like version of "The Wedding March."

I asked, "Wendy, can you keep your dress up long enough to walk down the aisle?"

"Not without holding the top up with both hands."

"What do you think, Jenny?" I asked.

She glanced down at the back of Wendy's wedding gown. "I've seen hospital gowns with more coverage. Hand me your jacket."

"What?" I asked as Wendy tugged at the bodice with both hands, trying to keep her bosom covered.

"I'm going to cover Wendy's backside by wrapping your coat over her shoulders."

"Here," Sparky said, "use mine."

He was about to release his hug when Jenny yelled, "No! Don't let go of Wendy!" She stepped behind me and slipped my coat off my shoulders, causing only moderate pain. Then she draped my coat over Wendy's back.

With my coat covering Wendy's gaping gown, and Sparky's hug keeping the wedding gown from falling to the floor, I looked at Jenny. "Now what?"

"The five of us are going to shuffle down the aisle in a group hug."

Grabbing Brian's collar, I pulled him into the hug, further blocking the view of Wendy's bosom. Jenny moved so her back was toward the crowd. "Okay, let's shuffle toward the back of the hall."

Chairs scraped as people moved to create enough space for the group to pass. Hulda, who'd been sitting on a shelf built into her walker, stood and asked, "What's going on? Are they consummating the marriage in the aisle?"

Karla Telker moved quickly to Hulda's side and whispered, "There's a problem with Wendy's gown."

"What's going on?" Hulda asked in an outdoor voice. "Are her boobs sticking out? I heard one of the firemen say something about her boobs."

"I think the zipper is stuck, or something," Karla said, hoping to quiet Hulda. "Let's check out the buffet. Okay?"

"I hope they have lime Jell-O with pears," Hulda replied. "It's not a wedding buffet without lime Jell-O."

As we neared the halfway point of our walk down the aisle, I heard fabric rip. "What was that?"

Jenny glanced down, then giggled. "We've got a 'plumber's butt' situation back here."

Wendy shuddered and said, "I feel a draft."

I leaned close to her and said, "Keep shuffling and don't let go of Sparky."

Brian chuckled.

"What?" I asked.

"There's a bear tattoo peeking out at me from the top of Wendy's gown."

"Ignore it. Look away."

"I can't," Brian replied. "It's one of those things that keeps you focused. A little more of him comes into view with each step."

"Wendy, pull up your top before Brian goes blind."

"I can't unsee him," Brian replied as Wendy tugged at her bodice.

"Stop!" Wendy cried out. "Someone is stepping on the hem. I can't keep the top up."

Jenny reached around Wendy to help adjust the dress. "The dress is too tight. There's nothing for me to grab."

"Grab it lower," Wendy suggested. "Under my tummy."

"Let me help," Brian said.

"Get your hand off my butt!" Wendy replied.

"Sorry, I thought I was grabbing..."

"Grabbing what, a water balloon?"

At the back of the lodge's hall, we stopped. "Now what?" I asked.

"Get one of the honor guards!" Sparky said. "They're wearing their fire gear. We can wrap Wendy in a fireman's coat and buckle her in."

Stella Hygge ran out the door and returned a moment later with her yellow rubberized fireman's coat. With Jenny's help, they pulled it over the bride's shoulders. Wendy pushed her arms into the coat in a deft move and Sparky pulled the front of the coat closed as the wedding gown fell to the floor.

Stifling a smile, Stella stepped back. "That was a close call."

"All right, step back and let me catch a breath," Wendy said. Her face was beet red, and her breathing came in short gasps.

Jenny put her arm over Wendy's shoulder and whispered to her. A second later, Wendy gasped and doubled over in pain. "OMG, that hurts!"

Jenny looked at me and said, "We need to take her to the hospital. The contractions that started during the ceremony are getting worse."

Sparky froze. "Contractions?"

"Wendy's in labor. The baby is coming," I said. "Get her into a car."

Stella stepped forward and took Wendy's elbow. "Forget a car. The rescue squad is right outside the door. Let's get you into it."

Chapter 18

After watching from the doorway as Stella and Jenny led Wendy out of the building, I moved to an empty table and took a seat. A moment later, I heard the rescue squad's siren start as they drove away.

Jenny returned, looking a bit haggard. She saw me and walked over. "You're as pale as a ghost," she said.

Brian overheard her and pulled a folding chair over to join us. "Are you okay, Doc?"

"He has a couple broken ribs," Jenny replied.

"It must've been a wild bachelor party," Brian responded.

"Yeah," I croaked, "and a long wedding."

"That was quite the ending, don't you think?"

"Thanks for picking up the pace as the safety pins started flying," Jenny said.

"It was either that or finish the ceremony in the ambulance."

As expected, the Whistling Pines residents were the first people in the wedding buffet line. Jenny looked at the people queueing up for the buffet and mused, "I wonder if the baby's birthday will be the same as the date on their marriage certificate?"

Brian thought, then said, "I don't suppose it makes a lot of difference as long as the wedding was before the birth."

I glanced at Sparky's mother, now at the head table, looking a bit worse for the wear. "I think the only person who cares is Sparky's mom."

A squawk came from the table where the first diners were eating, Hulda's distinctive voice rising over the general murmured conversations. "Who put shredded carrots in the orange Jell-O? Don't they know there are people here with dentures?"

Brian's eyes sparkled. "Just wait until she gets to the lemon poppyseed cupcakes."

I groaned as one of my intercostal muscles spasmed. Jenny turned to me and asked, "Do we need to take you home?"

"I'd rather sit a little longer before walking all the way to the car."

Digging into her purse, Jenny pulled out a prescription bottle and handed it to me. "I'll get you something to eat with a pain pill."

"I don't really need a narcotic," I said as Jenny walked away.

"I think you should listen to the nurse," Brian said.

"Yeah, she thinks that too."

Sherry approached our table and sat next to Brian. "Are you ready?" she asked.

Brian looked at me and asked, "Are you up for playing some music?"

"I'll pass. I'd want to sing and taking a deep breath isn't one of my superpowers today."

Sherry and Brian whispered like conspirators as they walked out of the door. A moment later, Jenny delivered a plate with a traditional church basement dinner scoop of wild rice hotdish, ham in a bun, a scoop of Jell-O with carrots, and a square of wedding cake.

"They cut the wedding cake without the bride?" I asked as I picked up the sandwich and took a bite.

"I suppose they reasoned there was no way Wendy would be back for the cake ceremony."

"Yeah, and it would kill a bunch of Swedes and Norwegians to let a perfectly good wedding cake go to waste."

"Where did Sherry and Brian go?"

"I think they're getting their instruments."

"What does Sherry play?"

"She's been refreshing her clarinet skills."

Brian and Sherry walked in with their instruments, then moved two chairs to the corner bandstand, while whispering to each other.

"What music would be appropriate for a clarinet and tuba?" Jenny asked.

As they raised their instruments, Brian started tapping rhythm with his foot. ““The Clarinet Polka,”” I replied as they started the familiar song.

Clarence Osterman walked in carrying an accordion and joined Brian and Sherry as they played the song the third time through. After a pause, they started the "Liechtensteiner Polka."

Several of the people sang the chorus, *"Ja, das ist ein Liechtensteiner polka mein Schatz..."*

Looking around at everyone singing, Jenny said, "It seems odd that a bunch of Scandinavians know the German words to that song."

"I'm sure they've heard it played at every dance since they were children."

Jenny pushed the prescription bottle toward my hand. "You really need one of these."

"Okay."

"I hate to medicate you too well. You'll start feeling better and want to be alongside them on the bandstand."

"Not today."

"Good choice. You're almost as green as the lime Jell-O."

A couple got up and started dancing, catalyzing a larger group to join them on the tiny dance floor.

"Sherry is having a good time," Jenny noted.

"I don't think the Svenska Gotters allowed her to socialize outside of church activities. She's blossoming."

Between songs, one of the young firemen brought Sherry a cup of punch and flirted with her. Jenny whispered, "You don't suppose the punch is spiked, do you?"

I looked toward the bar, where beer, wine, and mixed drinks were being served. "I'd say there's a pretty good chance there's alcohol in the punch."

Jenny stood and walked over to the bandstand. She whispered something that made Sherry set the punch aside, nodding her thanks to Jenny and then kept talking to the cute fireman.

Howard Johnson set a plate on the table and took the chair next to me. "How are you holding up, Doc?"

"I'm hoping the narcotics kick in soon so I can walk to the car."

Howard chuckled. "It's that bad, huh?"

"Oh, yeah. If I hadn't been the best man, I would've stayed home."

Howard unfolded his paper napkin and spread it across his lap. "I never thought I'd see Wendy in a wedding dress. She looked pleased."

"Right up until the safety pins let loose," I replied.

"That was quite a performance by the wedding party and the minister. You kept her covered. They whipped through the vows like pros."

"And then whisked her off to the hospital."

After taking a bite of his ham sandwich, Howard said, "And the second thing I'd never thought I'd see was Wendy having a baby. Love brings a lot of changes."

Jenny overheard the conversation and leaned close to me. "Most of them for the better," she said.

"Most?" I asked.

"Some husbands are stubborn and don't take direction well."

I stared at Howard and asked, "Why do women claim they love us for who we are, then immediately try to mold us into something else?"

"Peter, if you figure that out, you've solved the mystery of the ages."

Jeri and Lee Westfall joined us as the trio started playing "The Beer Barrel Polka."

"How are your ribs?" Lee asked.

"They're still sore. The nurse just dosed me with narcotics, so I should feel better pretty soon."

Lee's eyes twinkled. "You'll have to take Jeri for a spin around the dance floor."

"I've sworn off dancing and singing for the day."

Jeri nudged Lee's shoulder. "Quit teasing him. He's in pain."

As the music stopped, Hulda scolded, "Could you turn down the volume? We're trying to have a conversation over here."

Kathy, Karla, and Mary joined us. Karla shook her head as she sat. "I swear, Hulda sounds just like my mother. There's no filter between her brain and mouth."

Jenny reached out and touched my arm. "Are you ready to walk to the car?"

I took a breath that didn't hurt and nodded. Jenny helped me to my feet, and I smiled at our tablemates. "Have fun."

We eased through the crowd and walked outside into bright sunlight. "I wonder if Wendy's had her baby yet?" I asked as I approached the car.

"It's her first birth. She'll probably be in labor for hours."

"Poor Sparky," I said as Jenny helped me into the passenger seat.

"Poor Sparky? He's the one who got her into this condition."

"He had no idea what he was in for."

After buckling me in, Jenny kissed my forehead. "Did any of us know what we were in for?"

"I suppose not."

Jenny started the car and smirked.

"What?"

"What woman would ever have sex if you told her it could result in pushing a bowling ball out of her uterus?"

"I'm just saying..."

"You need to stop talking. The narcotics are interfering with your ability to reason through what you're saying."

Chapter 19

Monday morning

After drawing a mug of coffee from the urn, I turned and saw a half dozen hands waving to me from around the dining room. At the nearest table, Dolores patted the empty chair next to her. "Tell us about Wendy's baby."

Jeri Westfall nodded emphatically. "Yes, everyone wants to know about Wendy."

"I imagine you all know she had a baby boy yesterday morning."

Gladys Paulson wrinkled her nose. "We heard *that*. What's his name? How much does he weigh? How big is he?"

The rattling of a walker preceded pain in my shin when Hulda banged into me. "Forget all the statistics. I want to know if Wendy screamed. Could you hear her from outside of the hospital? Wendy always struck me as a screamer with a low pain threshold."

"Oh, Hulda, they have pain control things, blocks and such, so childbirth isn't the experience it was when we were having children," Kathy chided.

"Spill it, Peter," Hulda urged. "Was Wendy a screamer?"

"I think Wendy held up very well. Sparky Junior was born without screaming or injury to the father. He weighed six pounds, eleven ounces, and was nineteen inches long."

"Bah!" Hulda declared. "They should've left him in the womb another couple of weeks until he was a real keeper. I really appreciate the ten-pound babies who show up looking ready for kindergarten."

With her pronouncement completed, Hulda swung her walker around, striking knees, chairs, and table legs. As she left, Gladys said, "Hulda is such an unhappy person. I pray for her every week."

"What do you pray for?" Karla asked.

"Laryngitis."

The reply was unexpected and out of character. Having caught me halfway through a swallow, I choked painfully and wiped my face with a napkin. "That was precious," I replied.

"What's going on with your antique dealer's cache?" Dolores inquired.

"They're trying to identify the blood on the knife."

"Do you know if the blood belonged to the Crazy Norwegian?" Jeri asked.

"We suspect it's his blood, but there's no way to verify that without finding one or more of his relatives."

"Find the kid he had with Astrid Tostenrud," Dolores said.

I turned to look at her, as did her tablemates and the women from the adjoining table. "Astrid had a kid with the Crazy Norwegian?"

"It was common knowledge back in 1951. Eugene was off fighting in Korea, and Astrid got pregnant while she was fooling around with the Crazy Norwegian. Her family made up a story about her getting sick and spending six months in Minneapolis. We all knew she'd been knocked up and had a baby boy she gave up for adoption."

"Did anyone tell this to the police when the Crazy Norwegian disappeared?"

"Why would we?" Dolores asked. "He died on the lake."

"He might've been killed and dumped in the lake."

"It doesn't make any difference. His body was never found, so there's never been a murder to investigate."

"No one suspected Eugene Tostenrud's involvement in the disappearance?"

Dolores snorted. "*Everyone* suspected Eugene. But they never found the Crazy Norwegian's body."

"Who is Astrid's son?" I asked.

The ladies looked among themselves, unable to come up with an answer. "We don't know," Dolores answered. "Like I said, he was born in Duluth, and Astrid gave him up for adoption."

Trying my best sly smile, I said, "But you suspect you know his identity. Right?"

"You should ask Ginny Johnson. She and Astrid were best friends back in the day."

"Ginny is in the memory care unit. She might not be the most reliable source of information."

Dolores patted my arm. "Ginny can't remember your name, but she can recite things that happened in grade school."

"There must be someone else who knows," I protested.

"There is," Dolores replied. "But you'll need a séance to contact Eugene of Astrid Tostenrud."

Easing myself back from the table while grimacing in pain, I weighed the prospect of discussing the past with Ginny versus any other leads I had.

Hesitating as I stood at the table, Karla reached over and tapped my shoulder. "You know, a séance might be fun."

"Wasn't your husband a Baptist minister? I'd think séances would be in the same category as witchcraft, drinking, and playing cards."

Kathy shook her head. "A séance is like playing with the Ouija board. Everyone knows it's all make-believe."

Dolores cleared her throat. "The Baptists don't believe my old house is haunted either. How is the ghost in the organ room, Peter?"

"He's been remarkably quiet since we turned it into a nursery." As soon as I'd said the words, Karla, Mary, and Kathy all looked surprised. "He was a friendly ghost. He'd just play the organ once in a while," I said.

"But he's stopped since you moved the baby into that room?" Mary asked.

"Pretty much so. I can't recall him playing at all since Amy came home from the hospital."

"I'm not surprised," Dolores opined. "I think she was lonely. She's probably happy to have a baby in that room."

"The séance should be at your house," Kathy suggested, "especially since it's already haunted."

"We're not having a séance at my house. Besides, I don't know a medium."

Mary nodded. "I'll bet your tuba-playing friend knows a medium. Tuba players consort with all sorts of shady people."

Sherry motioned for me from the dining room door. I gladly ended the séance discussion to see what she needed. "What's going on?"

"I'm sorry to interrupt your conversation, but we've got a singalong scheduled. Wendy's at the hospital. Do you want to cancel it?"

"You and I can lead the singing."

"I don't know many popular songs from the era when the residents were young."

"Pull up the Great American Songbook on your computer and chose songs from the '30s to '60s"

"The '60s is the Beatles era, right?"

"Good idea. Let's do a Beatles medley."

Sherry lit up. "I'll look up a few songs I know and print out the words." She paused. "Do you need the chords?"

"I've played all of them. The chords will come to me."

Sensing that Sherry was about to dash away, I asked, "Have you ever been to a séance?"

"The Svenska Gotters consider séances the Devil's work. We weren't allowed to discuss or be involved in that kind of thing."

"So, you personally, have never been to a séance?"

"Off the record?"

"Sure, off the record."

"My freshman roommate was into all kinds of paranormal stuff. She thought our room in an off-campus house was haunted, so she held a séance to meet with the ghost, hoping to persuade him to move on."

"What happened?"

"It was surreal, like something out of a horror movie. We did the séance during a thunderstorm. Every time Madyson asked a question, either thunder would rumble or the lights would flash."

"Did Madyson banish the ghost?"

"I guess."

"Is she still around Duluth?"

"I haven't seen Maddy in a while, but she might be. Do you want me to find her?"

"Yeah. If you find her, ask if she'd be willing to do a séance in my haunted house."

"Your house is haunted? Really?"

"The organ sometimes plays when there's no one in the room."

"Is it cool, or scary?"

"It's mostly annoying. I haven't heard the music since we brought Amy home and turned that room into a nursery."

* * *

Back in my office, I punched Kerry's number into the phone. "What's up?"

"Did you get the DNA results from the knife?"

"No one's called or emailed them to me."

"Dolores told me that Astrid had a son while her husband was in Korea. According to her, the Crazy Norwegian was the baby's father. Astrid moved to Duluth for a few months to have the baby, then put him up for adoption. Some of the residents are sure Eugene killed the Norwegian over the affair."

"Great! I love when your rumors close murder cases. Who should I list as the key witness who saw Eugene killing the Norwegian?"

"No one saw Eugene kill him. But they know he did it."

"Perfect! Another murder solved without a witness or evidence. I love it."

"I don't need your sarcasm."

Kerry chuckled. "Then you shouldn't call to tell me a murder has been solved based on the recollections of old women who are passing rumors."

264

"I think we're going to hold a séance to identify Astrid's love child."

Snorting, Kerry said, "Man, I don't know how this call can get any better."

"Do you have any better ideas?" I asked.

"Like I said the last time we spoke, I've moved on to crimes where the victim and perpetrator are still alive."

"Do you have any open murder cases?"

"About half a dozen."

"Let me rephrase that. Do you have any *recent* murder cases?"

"No, but there are a couple of burglaries and an assault."

"What about Astrid's murder?"

"It was a tragic accident caused by a colorblind person hooking up the wrong tank. No prosecutor would touch that case."

"Do you want to attend a séance?"

"Are you nuts? If I did that, every defense attorney who cross-examined me for the rest of my career would question my judgment."

Suddenly aware that the wheels were turning and there was going to be a séance at my home, I asked, "Can Jenny visit your house with our kids during the séance?"

"Tell her to bring a bottle of wine. I'll make popcorn."

Brian stepped into my office as I ended the call with Kerry. "I heard you're having a séance. I'd like to help."

Sensing an ulterior motive, I asked, "Why?"

"What would be spookier than tuba music coming from an upstairs room?"

"We already have an organ-playing ghost. I don't want to stretch that into a demonic band."

Uninvited, Brian plopped down in my guest chair. "What's your plan?"

"I'm going to have a séance, and we're going to find Astrid's love child."

Brian nodded as if he was convinced. "You *do* know that's an unlikely outcome. Most séances contact a third-party ghost who tries to connect with the target ghost."

"You seem to know a lot about séances."

"I watched a lot of old movies when I was a kid. A séance was a staple of about half the classic horror mysteries. You'll need someone to make the lights flicker, and maybe cause a ghostly apparition to hover in a corner."

"Are you volunteering?"

"As hard as it may be for you to believe, I was an engineer in a previous life. I am capable of producing all sorts of special effects given enough time and money."

"I have no budget and the séance is tonight."

"Geesh, Doc. You've got to give me a little notice."

I turned to my computer and entered my password. After a quick internet search, I printed the photo from Astrid's obituary. I handed it to Brian. "Can you make her appear in the corner of my dining room?"

"Is there a window near the table?"

"There's one at the end of the dining room."

"Consider it done."

"How about flickering lights?" I asked.

"Do you have fuses or circuit breakers?"

"It's an old house, so we have screw-in fuses."

"That's a little tricker, but I should be able to rig up a solenoid. Do you want flickering or a total outage?"

"Total darkness," I replied. "I want to flip the switches and have nothing happen."

"How will I know when you want the special effects?"

"My phone has a walkie-talkie app. Download it, and you can listen in on the whole séance."

"Give me some nonsense words so I know when to queue up the special effects."

"I'll have the medium call for Astrid. The third time she calls Astrid's name, make her appear."

"How about the power outage?"

"I'll cough three times."

"Got it. Astrid three times and three coughs for lights out." Brian stood. "Is your house unlocked? I'll grab my bag of tricks and work out the electrical failure right away."

"I haven't found a key for the house, so it's always unlocked."

Brian smirked.

"What?" I asked.

"You've become a real Two Harborite."

"Huh?"

"All the city folks hire a locksmith as soon as they buy a house here. You're okay leaving your house unlocked, like most of the locals."

"Maybe I'm too broke to hire a locksmith."

Shaking his head, Brian asked, "What time does the séance start?"

Sherry stuck her head around the corner. "Maddy is excited about playing the medium again."

"What time can she get here?" I asked.

"Her shift at the brewery ends at five. By the time she changes and drives to Two Harbors, it'll be at least seven o'clock."

I nodded to Brian. "Let's plan on starting at eight o'clock."

"Who's your target?"

"Kathy, Mary, Karla, and Ginny all seem to know something about Astrid's disappearance, the birth of her child, and the baby's adoption. I suspect that Astrid's nephew, Doctor Robertson, knows something, too. I'm going to get them all in the same room. We'll see what happens."

With Brian gone, Sherry sat in my guest chair. "Will those people come to a séance?"

"I'm sure they'll all be curious enough to attend."

Sherry bit her lower lip. "Can I come, too?"

"Of course! Come with Maddy."

Sherry perked up and stood. "I think the people are gathering for the Beatles show."

I handed Sherry my guitar case. "Tune the guitar and stall for a bit. I have to invite a dentist to the séance."

Dr. Robertson wasn't thrilled about the prospect of driving to Two Harbors after dark, but he agreed to come, enticed by the thought of finding out the name of his cousin. I was about to dash off when I was struck by a rare moment of husbandly lucidity. I called Jenny, "Um, dear. We're hosting a séance tonight."

"What?"

"Deb and Kerry have invited you and the kids over for the evening. He suggested you bring a bottle of wine."

"Back up. What séance?"

"I've got a bunch of people coming over to our house for a séance. We're going to contact Astrid Tostenrud's ghost."

"Who is attending this séance?"

"I've invited Karla, Mary, Kathy, and Ginny."

"Really? They're willing to attend an evening séance?"

"Absolutely!" I lied.

"Are you going to banish our organ-playing ghost?"

"No, I think we're going to reveal the identity of Astrid Tostenrud's son."

"How?"

"Through the power of the medium."

"Speaking of that, who is your medium?"

"Sherry has a friend who did a séance when they were in college. Maddy succeeded in chasing a ghost out of their spooky rental house."

"Are you serious?"

"I've enlisted Brian Johnson who's going to create some special effects to help move things along."

"I'll call Deb Stone and suggest that I buy everyone supper before imposing on them for the evening."

"That's probably a good plan. I'm not sure how long it will take Brian to set up his special effects."

* * *

The community room was nearly full when I entered. Sherry was sitting on a stool in the front and tuning my guitar while talking with the people seated nearby. I noticed the song sheets in everyone's hands as I walked to the front of the room. Sherry had been busy.

"Hi folks," I said, accepting the guitar from Sherry. "Is everyone ready to sing along with some Beatles songs?"

As is often the case, the response was more of a quiet Scandinavian, "yes" than a boisterous, "YES!"

"I see that Sherry handed out the lyrics to some songs, which is first?"

Someone from the back of the room called out, "I Wanna Hold Your Hand."

I strummed three chords, then Sherry and I sang, "Oh yeah, I'll tell you somethin'…" The residents joined in, their voices getting stronger when we got to the familiar chorus.

"All My Loving," came next. As Sherry got more confident, she sang harmony in the chorus, which brought smiles from the residents.

After half an hour, we'd completed all the printed song lyrics. Sherry handed me a water bottle and as I took a drink, someone said, "How about that song from the movie, *Ghost*.

I turned to Sherry and asked, "Do you know "Unchained Melody?"""

"Sort of. I know the opening verse and the chorus."

I picked the intro, then nodded to Sherry who sang, "Oh, my love, my darling…"

I joined her in the chorus, then I sang the second verse. We ended by singing a duet of the chorus with a half dozen voices joining in from the audience. When we finished, I stood and thanked everyone. As I packed my guitar, Karla, Mary, and Kathy, who'd been three of the strongest singalong voices, came forward.

Mary looked troubled. "I don't believe in séances."

Karla nodded her agreement. "I think they're smoke and mirrors."

Kathy smiled. "I think a seance sounds like fun." When the others glared at her, she replied, "I just like the idea of getting out for a night and doing something different."

"Work with me on this," I said. "I hope to identify Astrid's son."

Karla squirmed. "Let sleeping dogs lie."

"I'd like to solve the Crazy Norwegian's disappearance."

"What time should we be there?" Mary asked.

"We're going to start at eight."

Kathy chuckled. "Ooh, a late night. Eight is past my bedtime."

Chapter 20

I arrived home about six o'clock and found Sparky and Brian in my kitchen. "Why aren't you at the hospital, Sparky?"

"The baby is sleeping, and I was superfluous."

"Superfluous?" I asked, surprised. Sparky was an educated professional, but his vocabulary rarely used words not found on a sixth-grade spelling test.

"That's what Wendy said. The baby needed her, and she needed the nurses. No one really needed me, making me superfluous."

"What did you choose for the baby's name?"

I could tell from Sparky's grimace that wasn't a pleasant topic. "We're undecided."

"What name did you want?"

"I suggested Victor, after my uncle."

Brian snorted, trying to stifle his laughter.

"What name does Wendy want?"

"She's leaning toward Tyler, as in Steven Tyler."

"I suppose Tyler wouldn't be a bad choice," I replied. "Wendy is a big Aerosmith fan."

"Yeah, Wendy is into anything musical. He's also a screamer, like Tyler."

 Has your mother visited the baby?" I asked.

"She was there, but she and Wendy argued about how to hold the baby, so Mom left."

"Sparky has been helping me with the electrical special effects," Brian said.

Nodding, Sparky added, "I was an electrician's apprentice, which is where I picked up the nickname. That was before I got into computers."

Brian pulled out what appeared to be a garage opener remote control. Dramatically pushing the button, he smiled, but nothing happened. "Wait for it." After a few seconds, the lights all went out.

Pressing the remote again caused the electricity to restart. "I'm impressed," I said.

Reaching for what looked like a camcorder, Brian pointed it at the cupboards and pushed a button. I found myself staring at Astrid's picture, with waves flowing through her features, making the image eerie. "Sparky added some special effects. I thought just projecting Astrid's image on the window would be boring." A second later, Astrid's hand rose, and her lips started moving as if speaking.

Nodding excitedly, Sparky said, "I used an artificial intelligence program on the photo to animate it. Astrid's lips will be moving when she speaks through the medium, and she'll gesture with her hands."

"That's great, guys."

"Sparky's going to hang out with me. We're controlling the special effects from his house."

Looking at the dining room table, I realized it wasn't big enough to seat everyone I expected to attend. "My ribs are banged up. Could you guys put the leaf in the dining room table and bring a couple of chairs down from the second floor?"

Sparky and Brian inserted the leaf into the dining room table, so it would seat eight. Then they carried additional chairs from upstairs as I dimmed the lights in the rest of the house. By 7:45 we had everything in place, and Sparky and Brian left. After a few minutes, I called Brian. "Are you set?"

"We're as ready as we're going to be," he replied.

"Someone's knocking at the door," I said. "We'll be starting soon."

"Roger, wilco, and out," Sparky replied.

Rolling my eyes, I thought, *I haven't heard anyone say, roger, wilco, and out since I rode with the search and rescue helicopter crew in Iraq.* I wondered if Sparky knew that meant the transmission is received, will cooperate, and I'm through speaking. Maybe he did, since he used them in the proper context? *Sparky, you're full of surprises*, I thought.

Placing the phone in my pocket, I went to the door and ushered in Karla, Kathy, and Mary. "Ladies, you're the first to arrive."

Kathy stepped into the kitchen and said, "We're Scandinavian farmers. We were taught it was better to be an hour early than a minute late."

"That's a rarity these days," I replied.

I was closing the door when I felt resistance. Stepping back, Maddy and Sherry rushed into the kitchen. "Our medium and her able assistant have arrived."

Sherry peeked out of the door furtively before closing it. "Don't tell anyone I'm her assistant. Or that I'm even here. My father would *not* be happy to hear that I'd been at a séance."

I nodded my understanding. "My lips are sealed. On the other hand, we'll have a bunch of gossiping senior citizens arriving soon. They aren't known for keeping secrets."

Sherry thought for a second, then replied, "If it comes out, I'll tell Dad they confused me with someone else. His congregation is mostly confused, forgetful retirees. He'll want to accept that explanation."

I was surprised when Ginny Johnson arrived with Jeri Westfall. "Ladies, I'm pleased that you're here."

Jeri smiled, and said, "Ginny needed a ride. I offered to drive her here because I thought a séance might be fun."

A step behind them was Dr. Robertson, looking less pleased about the séance than Ginny and Jeri. "Can we get the show on the road? I don't like driving in the dark. And I certainly don't want to be driving around when the drunks are on the road after the bars close."

Ushering everyone to the dining room, I gestured for Maddy to take the seat at the head of the table, her back to the window. I put Dr. Robertson opposite her, with Ginny to his right and Jeri to his left. I seated Kathy, Karla, and Mary around the table, separated by Maddy, Sherry, and me.

After switching off the kitchen and living room lights, I left the light fixture on over the dining room table. The glowing numerals on the microwave and the stove cast an eerie blue aura. As I sat, the others stopped talking and focused on Maddy, outfitted like a Gypsy. She wore a peasant blouse and a loose, flowing skirt with a wide sash around her waist. Her hair was wrapped in a kerchief and her makeup was garishly overdone.

With everyone staring at Maddy, the room became silent except for the ticking of the old wind-up grandfather clock left behind by Dolores when she gave the house to Jenny and me. Maddy closed her eyes and reached her hands to the sides. "Everyone join hands."

We all took the hands of the people on either side of us. Ginny, who was a few cards short of a 52-card deck asked, "Is this sanitary? Is that Covid thing over?"

She was shushed by Karla and Mary.

Maddy drew a deep breath and tipped her head back. "We're here to speak with the spirit of our beloved Agnes."

"Astrid," I hissed.

Maddy's eyes opened for a second and I mouthed, "Astrid."

Closing her eyes, she went on, "We're here to speak with the spirit of our beloved *Astrid*. Are you with us tonight, Astrid?"

I coughed three times, signaling Brian.

"Covid!" Ginny shrieked.

Over the phone, Brian whispered, "Was that the signal?"

Other than Maddy, every head turned toward me, trying to discern the source of the male whisper. I looked around, trying to act as confused by the voice as the rest. Then I coughed three more times.

This time, Sparky whispered to Brian, "He coughed."

Before anyone could look for that voice, the dining room lights went out and the room was plunged into darkness. Ginny shrieked, "It's Astrid!"

"Oh, for pity's sake. Peter, turn the lights back on," Robertson said.

I stood up and walked to the light switch. I clicked it on and off several times before returning to the table. "Nothing," I whispered.

"Astrid, come to us," Maddy called. "Astrid. Astrid. Astrid."

"What the hell?" Robertson said when Astrid's image appeared on the window, the rippled old glass added to the eerie waviness of the projected image. Hearing Robertson, several of the women followed his gaze toward the window, causing them to gasp.

"Who was the father of your child?" Maddy implored. "What happened to your baby?"

Floorboards creaked upstairs, raising goosebumps on my arms because I knew no one was up there. A moment later, the organ started playing "Over the Rainbow."

Sherry's eyes were wide, and she appeared ready to run for the door if not for the two people holding her hands. The organ's volume increased as it played the melody a second time.

Maddy's wailing gained intensity. "What happened to your son, Astrid?" Her body spasmed and jerked. I wondered if she was having a medical emergency until in an unfamiliar voice she said, "I gave Clifford to my sister to raise." As Maddy spoke, Astrid's lips moved as if speaking, and her right hand gestured toward the group.

All of the women looked at the dentist, who seemed as shocked by the information as any of them.

Maddy continued, as if in a trance, "I was in no condition to raise a bastard child with my husband in Korea."

"Wait! Who is my father?" the dentist asked, now fully into the séance.

"I was weak. The Norwegian was so handsome..."

Maddy's apparent trance ended, as did the organ music. A moment later, the electricity came on, lighting the dining room and making the microwave beep. Astrid's face disappeared from the window.

"Wait!" Roberston shouted. "Ask her about the treasure. Do I inherit it because I'm her son?"

"What happened to the Crazy Norwegian? Did Eugene kill him?" Karla asked.

Maddy pitched forward, either exhausted from the séance, or putting on a great show.

I turned to Robertson. "You didn't know you were Astrid's child?"

"Honest to God, I thought Astrid and Eugene were my aunt and uncle." The women grilled him about his parentage and the death of his biological father.

Sherry skirted the women and whispered to me, "The organ scared the poop out of me. You could've warned me."

Maddy was a step behind Sherry. "I heard footsteps and then the organ started playing. That was incredible, Peter."

I nodded toward the stairs. "Come on. There's no one up there."

I led the two young women up the stairs to the dark hallway. Flipping on the lights, I led them to the nursery where the old organ sat in the corner of the room. The piano bench was pushed under the keyboard, and both were dusty. I wiped my finger across the keys and showed Maddy and Sherry the dust. "There aren't any fingerprints on the keys."

Sherry shivered. "Then how?"

I leaned over the keyboard and played the familiar opening of Bach's "Fugue in G minor," popularized in many horror films of the black and white movie era. Stepping back, I gestured for Sherry to inspect the keyboard.

"Only the keys you've just played have fingerprints on them."

Maddy was out of the room as if shot by a cannon. Sherry and I followed along behind. Just before I got to the nursery's door, Sherry stopped and pointed at an assortment of musical instrument cases. "Do you play all of those?"

"Yes, to varying degrees."

"You should bring the accordion to work sometime. We could invite Brian and have a polka dance for the residents."

"I'd need a lot of practice before I'm ready to play the accordion in front of an audience."

We walked downstairs and into the dining room, where people milled around, asking questions and visiting.

Dr. Robertson approached me and asked, "What's going to happen to the crown that was inside the footlocker?"

"I assume the State Department will return it to the Korean government. It's a national treasure."

"If not for Uncle Eugene caring for the crown, it would've been taken by the North Koreans and probably sold to finance their army. Eugene probably saved it."

"I'm afraid your Uncle Eugene wasn't known for his altruism."

"Still, there should be a finder's fee."

I nodded. "I agree that the Silver Bay and Two Harbors libraries are due a finder's fee."

Robertson frowned and walked away.

Chapter 21

I made Kerry buy doughnuts, and then we picked up the Two Harbors librarian before driving to Silver Bay. In a library conference room, we ate doughnuts and drank coffee while Kerry and I explained what had happened since the footlocker was unearthed.

Shannon asked, "Do you think we might actually get a finder's fee from the Koreans?"

Kerry shrugged. "Our State Department is talking with them. That decision will be made far above my pay grade as the lowly police chief."

A professionally dressed woman walked into the meeting room and put her hands on her hips. "All right, who brought doughnuts and forgot to invite me?"

I offered the doughnut bag to her. "You are?"

Taking a doughnut and setting it on a napkin, the woman offered her hand to Kerry and then to me. "I'm Lana, the Silver Bay City Manager. The organization chart says I'm Shannon's boss. I'm not so sure who's bossing whom most days." After taking a bite of her doughnut, she added, "By the way, I get to go along on the next treasure hunt.”

Shannon was effusive with praise. “Peter is the one who figured it out and stayed with the search. Tell Lana about the ghostly organ music.”

I repeated the story about the unexplained organ music playing during the séance, as well as the plan to have the lights going out and the dead woman’s face projected on the window.

“You should come to the Silver Bay Library for a Halloween program next year,” Shannon suggested.

“I think I’m stuck in Two Harbors with my own trick-or-treaters. I can suggest a Halloween trip to my tuba player and special effects man. They were the stars of the séance.”

In unison, Lana and Shannon said, “Do that!”

* * *

When I walked down for coffee the next day, Brian was sitting at a dining room table with Karla, Mary, and Kathy. The women were laughing, making me suspect Brian had just told his latest tuba joke. I slid over a chair from an adjoining table and joined them.

Karla put her hand on my arm. “You two should put on a séance for Whistling Pines. It was like going to the haunted house at the state fair. Everyone knew it was all in fun, but it gave us chills anyway."

Mary rolled her eyes. "I'm not sure our pastor would've approved, but it was fun."

Looking at Brian, I asked, "When did you rig the organ?"

"I didn't do anything to the organ."

"It played "Over the Rainbow" just before the end of the séance."

"That wasn't my doing."

Sherry walked over to the table and overheard Brian's denial. "Yeah, I went upstairs with Peter and Maddy. The organ keys were still covered with dust. It must've been controlled by something inside the organ itself."

Brian continued to protest his innocence. "Really. Sparky and I just rigged the lights and projected the face on the window. We never went to the second floor."

I slid my chair away from the table and looked around the dining room. Spotting Dolores sipping coffee with Jeri Westfall, I walked over and said, "We had a séance at the house last night."

Dolores nodded. "I heard. Ginny Johnson spilled the beans about Clifford Robertson being Astrid's illegitimate son."

Taking a chair, I asked, "Did you know that?"

"Well, it was common knowledge. But you know how that works, just because someone tells you about a rumor like that, doesn't make it the truth."

"Is it true, or was it just a rumor?"

"Ginny was close to Astrid. If Ginny relayed that information, I assume it's true."

"Did you hear about the lights going out, Astrid's face in the window, and the organ playing?"

Jeri nodded and said, "I told Dolores about those eerie things happening. It made for a great show."

"The organ played on its own," I said. "No one touched it."

Dolores stared at me. "Of course someone played it."

"There was no one upstairs and the keys were still dusty."

Dolores replied, "Agnes played for you."

"Agnes?"

"She's the ghost."

I sighed. "We have a ghost named Agnes?"

"She was the previous owners' nanny. The rumor is that she got pregnant and hanged herself in the basement."

"You never told me about a ghost who hung herself."

Dolores frowned. "Peter, use proper English. Pictures are hung. People are hanged."

"You never told me about someone who *hanged* herself in the basement."

"It's just a rumor. I didn't feel the need to repeat it."

"But you knew the organ sometimes played by itself?"

"You told me that it happened the Christmas you moved into the house. It shouldn't have been a surprise."

"Why do you think the organ started playing during the séance?" I asked.

"Did someone call the ghost's name?" Dolores asked.

"Maddy called for Astrid to appear," I replied.

Jeri put her hand on my arm. "Don't you remember? The medium said, 'Agnes' the first time she called for the ghost. You corrected her."

Brian joined us at the table. "Have we solved the organ mystery?"

Dolores seemed surprised. "There's no mystery. You called Agnes, and she started playing the organ. I assume she played something from her repertoire. Was it a song from the 1930s?"

""Over the Rainbow.""

"I suppose *The Wizard of Oz* was released about the time Agnes killed herself."

"There you go, Doc," Brian said. "Your ghost mystery is solved."

Walking back to my office, I asked Brian, "What are the odds that Clifford Robertson is really the Crazy Norwegian's son?"

"That can be verified by DNA testing."

"Did Robertson murder Astrid or was it just a tragic accident?"

"You're the detective. I'm just a tuba player."

"Police use the term *local knowledge* when tapping into information known only by people in the area. I thought you might have a non-obvious insight that Kerry and I might miss."

"Why would Dr. Robertson kill his aunt? It's not like he was trying to torture her to expose the location of the puzzle box. I think he made an honest mistake because he's colorblind."

"But he tried to cover it up."

"He was embarrassed after he discovered the mistake."

Accepting Brian's argument, I said, "That still leaves the Crazy Norwegian's death unsolved."

"You don't believe that Eugene Tostenrud was upset about his wife getting knocked up while he was overseas?"

"He's not the first soldier or sailor to come home to a baby fathered by someone else while stationed overseas or on a ship."

"Eugene was a bully. Anyone who sold or bought antiques from him suspected they'd been cheated. I wouldn't be surprised that he'd kill his wife's lover. I'm sure Astrid also paid a price for her infidelity." Brian paused as we arrived at my office. "When the BCA compares Dr. Robertson's DNA with the blood on the Korean knife, they'll probably be able to solve both the Crazy Norwegian's murder and the question of Robertson's paternity."

I closed my office door and called Kerry. After talking through the séance, we moved to the topic of DNA testing.

"I can request DNA from Dr. Robertson, but I'm not sure it's worth the cost and time to answer those questions. Besides, without the Crazy Norwegian's DNA, we're just speculating on the outcome."

"We're not looking for evidence that will prove a case *beyond a reasonable doubt*. We're just trying to answer the questions to satisfy our own curiosity."

"I can't spend the taxpayers' money to satisfy your curiosity."

"Call Dr. Robertson and explain our suspicions to him. I bet he'll pay for the DNA testing to answer his own questions about his parentage."

* * *

While Jenny put Amy to bed, I stared into space, pondering the information bouncing around inside my head. Jenny turned on the dining room lights. "Are you okay? Why are you sitting here in the dark?"

"How do you feel about having an organ-playing ghost named Agnes living in our house?"

After considering the question momentarily, Jenny said, "She doesn't seem to be a mean or destructive spirit."

"I guess she's not a poltergeist. She's only shown up a couple of times and only to play the organ."

"I can live with that; I think she adds character to our house. It'll probably be a selling point."

We were gently embracing, not around my ribs, when our back door burst open startling both Jenny and me. Sparky stepped in looking frantic. "Come quick!"

"What's the matter?" I asked.

"I just brought Wendy home and it's not going well."

"What's not going well?" Jenny asked.

"*Wendy's mother* just showed up. She accused *my mother* of raising a sex-crazed lunatic who took advantage of her little girl!"

Jenny started laughing. "Wendy's mother must live in a vacuum if she believes Wendy is an innocent young thing."

"Just come quick, or I'll have to call the cops!"

I took out my phone and dialed Kerry's cell phone. "You'd better rush over here. Wendy's mom is about to kill Sparky's mom."

Kerry sighed. "Can't you just walk next door and throw water on the two of them?"

"It sounds serious."

"Dial 911 if they start shooting at each other."

"You're not taking this seriously."

Kerry snorted. "It's difficult to be serious about anything related to Wendy and Sparky."

"There's an innocent child involved now."

Sighing again, Kerry said, "I'll have the dispatcher send an officer over."

"It might take someone with superior hostage negotiation skills."

"You mean, like me," Kerry replied.

"Right!"

"Fine. I'll put on pants and drive over."

Sparky looked at me expectantly and asked, "Is Kerry coming?"

"I think so. He said he was going to put pants on."

"What are we supposed to do until he arrives?"

"The Chief suggested throwing a bucket of water on them."

Sparky shook his head. "I don't think that would go well."

Jenny took Sparky's arm and led him out of the back door. "Let's see if we can separate them until Kerry arrives."

With them gone, I shook my head and looked at the stairway leading to the second-floor bedrooms. "What do you think, Agnes?"

The organ started playing softly, and the lyrics came to my lips, "Somewhere over the rainbow..."

The End

Other Dean Hovey books also published by BWL Publishing

Whistling Pines cozies
Whistling up a Ghost
Whistling Pirates
Whistling Bake Off
Whistling Artist
Whistling Fireman

Doug Fletcher mysteries
Stolen Past
Washed Away
Dead in the Water
Death in Shifting Sands
Devils Fall
Prairie Menace
Down River
Burnt Evidence
Gator Bait
Grave Survey
Dead End Trail
The Last Rodeo
Peril in Paradise
Western Justice
Strung Out to Die

Pine County Mysteries
Killer Secrets
Deadly Mixture
Fatal Business
Taxed to Death
Conflict of Interest

About the author

Dean Hovey is the award-winning and best-selling author of three mystery series. He uses his scientific background, travel, extensive research, and consultants to add reality and depth to his stories. One reader said his characters are like people he'd like to invite over for a beer and discussion.

Hovey's Doug Fletcher mysteries follow U.S. National Park Service investigators Doug and Jill Fletcher as their investigations take them to national parks from coast to coast. The Whistling Pines mysteries are humorous cozies set in a northern Minnesota senior residence, following Peter Rogers, the Whistling Pines recreation director, as he stumbles through the investigation of murders in his small town. The Pine County mystery series follows sheriff's deputies Pam Ryan, Floyd Swenson, and C.J. Jensen as they investigate murders in rural Minnesota.

Dean and his wife split their year between northern Minnesota and Arizona.

BWL Publishing

bwlpublishing.ca